_"Go on, ta_

Ethan's hand was a few inches from Nicole's nose, and the only way she could think to get rid of him was to smell it and shut him up. One sniff could put to rest—for good—the possibility that some exotic lust potion was on the loose in San Diego.

She edged her nose closer by an inch and inhaled deeply. There was no scent, save that of Ethan.

Then a white flash blinded Nicole for a split second, and a crazy-hot image flashed in her mind. Bare limbs intertwined, a woman's legs wrapped around a man's narrow hips—and their faces rapt with pleasure...

It was her and Ethan.

She shook the image out of her head and looked at Ethan. Their gazes locked. She felt herself moving forward, felt a burst of pure pleasure as Ethan came closer.

Nicole couldn't imagine why she'd mostly been able to resist him until now.

He was irresistible.

Blaze™

Dear Reader,

Working with Colleen Collins and Carrie Alexander to create the LUST POTION #9 miniseries gave me more than a few laughs, and also a few challenges as we tried to decide exactly how our lust potion would work (really well!), what the side effects would be (careful what you wish for...) and how our characters would stumble upon and use the world's most powerful aphrodisiac. Brainstorming with two such talented authors whose work I've always admired challenged me creatively, and I know my own writing was improved thanks to their input. Because of that and so much more, I am thrilled to have been included in this project.

I hope you fall in love with the LUST POTION #9 series. Look for Colleen's book, *A Scent of Seduction*, in November 2006, and Carrie's book, *A Taste of Temptation*, in December 2006. And don't forget to drop me a note at jamie@jamiesobrato.com to let me know what you thought of *A Whisper of Wanting*. You can learn more about me and my upcoming books on my Web site, www.jamiesobrato.com.

Sincerely,

Jamie Sobrato

A WHISPER OF WANTING
Jamie Sobrato

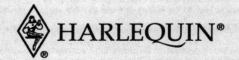

HARLEQUIN®

TORONTO • NEW YORK • LONDON
AMSTERDAM • PARIS • SYDNEY • HAMBURG
STOCKHOLM • ATHENS • TOKYO • MILAN • MADRID
PRAGUE • WARSAW • BUDAPEST • AUCKLAND

ISBN-13: 978-0-373-79288-7
ISBN-10:   0-373-79288-3

A WHISPER OF WANTING

This edition published by arrangement with Harlequin Books S.A.

® and TM are trademarks of the publisher. Trademarks indicated with
® are registered in the United States Patent and Trademark Office, the
Canadian Trade Marks Office and in other countries.

www.eHarlequin.com

Printed in U.S.A.

ABOUT THE AUTHOR

Golden Heart Award-winning author Jamie Sobrato
lives in Northern California, where she is trying
to discover an aphrodisiac that works nearly as
well as Lust Potion #9. When she's not concocting
failed potions, she is busy at work on her next
Harlequin Blaze book. *A Whisper of Wanting* is her
eleventh novel.

Books by Jamie Sobrato

HARLEQUIN BLAZE

HARLEQUIN TEMPTATION

*It's All About Attitude

To Colleen and Carrie,
my fellow Lust Potion girls

1

"CRAZY PASSION, hot sex, multiple orgasms—you can have it all."

The whispered male voice came from somewhere in the vicinity of Ethan Ramsey's left elbow. He turned toward the sound and did a double take at the person standing next to him. It was a tiny lizard of a man, five feet tall at most. Raisin eyes and leathery skin framed a beak of a nose, and his bald head shone as if it had been waxed.

"You want *crazy-passion-hot-sex-multiple-orgasms*?" the man hissed again, his voice a little bolder now, but still reminiscent of the drug dealers in Amsterdam whispering "Ecstasy, ecstasy" on every street corner.

The raisin-eyed gaze darted between Ethan and his two co-workers standing a few feet away. The three had wandered into the little tourist trap shop called Jag's on their way back to the office from lunch, and this man, presumably, was Jag.

Maybe Ethan shouldn't have had that martini at lunch. He couldn't possibly have heard the man correctly. But he looked at Zoe Aberdeen and Kathryn Walters, both of whom were staring at the man as if they'd heard the same thing he had, and he knew he couldn't blame this weird tableau on vodka.

"Excuse me?" Ethan said, figuring he might as well know the truth of it.

"You, the two ladies," the man said, then glanced over each shoulder to make sure he wasn't being overheard, "you want *crazy-passion-hot-sex-multiple-orgasms.*"

Kathryn and Zoe were still staring, jaws agape now. The three of them had heard rumors that the place was hawking a fake aphrodisiac to tourists at an exorbitant price. Being the naturally curious journalists they were, they figured they'd better investigate, and since Zoe had claimed to be in search of a voodoo doll, here they were.

Yet somehow, this lizard of a man had still managed to catch them by surprise. He was like the human version of an Internet pop-up ad, the promise of the impossible in a tiny, annoying package.

Ethan cleared his throat and tried to think of an appropriate response to the idea of his having multiple orgasms with his heretofore platonic co-workers. Not that he hadn't engaged in his share of fantasies starring each of them, but hell, he'd also fantasized about having sex with pretty much every attractive female he knew. That didn't mean he was going to act on it.

Before he could respond though, the lizard man

spoke again. "Balam K'am-bi—it's the love potion of the Gods. From deep in the heart of the Yucatan peninsula comes this elixir that brings the world's greatest sexual experiences to the person who dares to use it."

Ethan glanced from Zoe to Kathryn again and caught them trying not to laugh. He wasn't the only one who'd had a martini with lunch—Zoe had, too. But Kathryn, as usual, had abstained.

"So what do you think, girls?" Ethan said. "Multiple orgasms for all?"

Zoe shot him an in-your-dreams look, then to the storekeeper she said, "How much for a bottle?"

"For a lovely lady like you, only fifty dollars."

Her perfectly arched brows shot up. "I'll give you ten bucks, tops."

The lizard man held up his hands and shook his head. "That's impossible. I pay forty dollars just to get one bottle into the U.S. I'm a working man, I have to—"

He lost his train of thought when he seemed to spot something over Zoe's left shoulder. Ethan followed the man's gaze to a police cruiser parking in front of the shop.

At that moment, Kathryn glanced at her watch. "Whoa, we're due back from lunch in, like, thirty seconds."

The shopkeeper instantly lost interest in trying to sell them his fake love potion. His gaze darting between them and the cops climbing out of the cruiser, he edged his way back as Ethan and his co-workers headed for the door.

"Oh, wait a sec, guys—I wanted to buy that voodoo doll with the pointy boobies," Zoe said, stopping as they reached the door.

Ethan and Kathryn loitered in the doorway, watching as two police officers surveyed the store-front, then headed for the entrance. By the time the cops reached the door, Zoe was hurrying after them with her bag containing the voodoo doll, and the three of them headed back to work, leaving the shopkeeper to deal with the cops.

"That little guy was seriously weird," Zoe said, inspecting the contents of her bag as they walked.

Kathryn shuddered. "There was something creepy about him. He reminded me of…"

"Lew from marketing?" Ethan offered, recalling the similarity between the two men's appearances.

"Yes!" the two women said simultaneously.

"I bet he has a forked tongue," Zoe said.

"Lew asked me out once," Kathryn said, wincing. "He wanted me to go to open mike night at some coffeehouse and listen to him read his haiku about global warming or something. It was bizarre."

"And you didn't jump on that fabulous opportunity? Are you insane?" Zoe said and laughed.

"Wow, the 'come listen to my haiku' pitch—I

haven't tried that one yet," Ethan said, pretending to be impressed with the idea.

"Don't," Kathryn said. "It's not exactly a turn-on."

Outside in the bright Southern California sunshine, Ethan felt a short pang of longing for London, where he'd grown up. It was mid-October for chrissake, and barely a hint of autumn taking hold. Not that he could complain about all the lovely bare-skinned American girls he got to admire in the warm weather.

And then another pang—a ridiculous wish that he'd grabbed that bottle of lust potion when he'd had the chance. Why he wanted it, he didn't dare guess.

Normally, Ethan didn't have to rely on much more than his crooked smile and a little old-fashioned Brit charm to get pretty much any girl he pleased out of her knickers, so he wasn't about to jump all over the offer of crazy-passion-hot-sex-multiple-orgasms in a bottle, but hey, he had to keep his journalistic interests in mind too. He'd love to have known what the hell was in the little bottle.

Probably a nice cocktail of tap water and piss.

"You're looking awfully mischievous all of a sudden," Kathryn said to him as they rounded the corner headed toward the newspaper offices.

Ethan shook himself out of his lust-potion-induced thoughts and shrugged. "Just wondering what it would be like to have a real lust potion. Imagine the trouble we could get into…."

"I don't want to imagine," Kathryn said. "A lust potion is the last thing I need right now, with my non-existent love life."

"Maybe you shouldn't have dissed Lew from marketing so quickly," Ethan offered, then stepped aside to avoid getting hit by a flailing female hand.

"That's exactly why you need something like that," Zoe said. "So you can relax and get laid!"

The trio made it back to work in record time thanks to Kathryn's type-A, hard-charging fast-walk, and they squeaked into their respective offices without anyone so much as noticing their tardiness. Ethan went to work hunting down sources for a drug-deal-gone-bad story he had due into production by six o'clock.

He prided himself on never getting a fact wrong and never turning in a story late. If he was easygoing and congenial in his personal life, he was the exact opposite in his professional life. As a journalist, he'd been called relentless, ruthless, even cutthroat. He was willing to go pretty damn far in the pursuit of the truth. It was one of those values he respected above all else—the only thing he'd ever found in life that he could see himself dying for.

Okay, so that sounded a little overdramatic. But on even the most routine stories such as the one he was working on today, lives could be saved with the truth.

The more the public knew about the illegal drug trade in San Diego, the more they could protect themselves against it. The more scumbags who had the light shone on their activities, the fewer of them who'd have an easy time of dealing in the future.

He believed in the power of truth and the written word, and he wrote his hundredth drug deal story with the same passion he'd have put into any other story. They were all important, so long as they were true.

His work was his life. He'd yet to meet a woman who could accept that, and so the women came and went from his bed rather quickly. And for the most part that was okay with Ethan. For the most part.

Looking over his notes, he came to a place where he couldn't understand what he'd scrawled on his notepad while interviewing a source. He picked up the phone and dialed the number he'd written at the top of the page. After a few rings, a man picked up with a surly "Hello."

"Kevin Brenner?" Ethan asked.

"Yeah, what do you want?"

"This is Ethan Ramsey at the *San Diego Times*. We talked yesterday about the story I'm writing, and I just need to clarify one thing from your comments."

Silence for a moment too long, and then, "Look man, my ass is on the line from talking to you once. I ain't doing it again."

Ethan bit his lip to keep from muttering a curse. He

took a guess at what he'd scrawled on the paper. It wasn't like him to make messy notes.

"My notes say Dorado wasn't present at the time of the deal. Is that correct?"

"Yeah, that's right. Now don't call me again."

Ethan heard a click on the line, and then he was disconnected. He hung up his phone and rewrote his illegible note carefully this time. Even with the thought still in his head, he always kept his original notes filed away to cover his ass later, just in case. But he had a gut sense about when people were telling the truth and when they were lying, and his gut never steered him wrong. He could hammer at a person relentlessly with his questions until he was sure he'd gotten every last detail they knew. He'd yet to need his filed-away notes, but he kept them nonetheless.

Three hours later, he was finishing up a rough draft of the story when Zoe appeared at his desk, wearing an inscrutable expression.

"Remember the guy from that tourist trap shop?" she asked.

Ethan shook himself out of his writing-mode trance. He hadn't given that creepy little man a thought since they'd left. "Mr. Hot-Sex-Multiple-Orgasm?"

"Check this out." She held up a small corked bottle identical to the one the man had tried to sell them. "He must have planted it on me. I found it in my purse just now when I was looking for some gum."

"Guess he knew a woman in desperate need of a lust potion when he saw one, eh?"

"Lust potion *my ass*."

"Love it when you talk dirty to me, babe."

"Could you be serious for a minute? Why would he stick this stuff he was trying to sell us a few minutes before in my bag? It doesn't make any sense."

Ethan pondered that for a moment. "You think it had something to do with the police showing up? Maybe to remove the evidence of his scam from the premises?"

Zoe shrugged. "Beats me, but that was my first guess. Or maybe he took pity on us, thinking we all had such obviously lousy love lives—"

"Speak for yourself."

She rolled her eyes at him. "You're such a guy. Maybe we should turn this bottle over to the police, you think?"

"Sure, why not. I could run it down to the precinct tonight, actually. I've got to stop there anyway to follow up on a story."

"Okay, I'll bring it right back to you. I want to play a little joke on Kathryn first, pretend I bought it for her."

"Put it on her desk with a little note that says, 'For you, multiple orgasms in a bottle.'"

She flashed a devious smile and disappeared.

A half hour later, he'd wrestled his story into a final draft when Kathryn appeared at his desk looking none too amused at the bottle she held in her hand.

"Ha. Ha," she said, deadpan. "I'm *so* amused."

He held up his hands in a gesture of surrender. "It wasn't me! Zoe's the one you should be glaring at."

"Whomever's to blame, you're not funny. Not one little bit."

She dropped the bottle on his desk, then tromped off, her lovely ass shaking as she went.

Alone, Ethan picked up the bottle and twirled it around, staring at the clear liquid within it. He removed the cork, which felt a little loose, and took a whiff of the stuff. It had no odor at all, which didn't exactly reinforce his water and piss theory, but didn't altogether refute it, either.

If he'd been a gambling man, he'd douse some on and see what happened. But now he realized the little man hadn't even told them how to use the stuff. Was the user supposed to drink it, wear it or sniff it? If it was a potion, didn't that mean it had to be drunk?

He hadn't a freaking clue.

And could he really blame his curiosity about the so-called potion on his journalistic interests alone?

He needed to get a grip and take the bottle over to the crime lab before a certain hot little cop he wanted to drop in on left for the day.

Nicole Arroyo—a woman he'd once had a chance with but had blown it in a huge way—haunted him. He'd always had a thing for women in positions of authority, starting with his nursery school teacher and getting more ambitious as he grew, but his attraction to Nicole was far more than that. And it was more than just the fact that she presented his biggest sexual challenge with her unwillingness to give him the time of day. It was that she was strong, and she didn't take any shit from anyone, and more than any woman he'd ever met, she knew her convictions. She believed in her work, which in its own way was a pursuit of truth, going hand in hand with justice.

Of all the women he'd have liked to impress, she was number one on his list, and yet she was probably less impressed with him than any other female in the known universe. Of course, he'd given her plenty of reason not to be impressed with him.

After that night two years ago, the outrageous flirtation, the thrill of catching her interest, the one drink too many, the drunken fumbling, the wilted erection, the one-night stand gone all wrong, he'd always ached for a second chance to show Nicole that he actually was a great lover.

That night had not been representative of his usual performance in bed—in fact it was the only time he'd ever not been able to get it up—and it had strictly been a side effect of the alcohol. He wanted her to know that, and to know that it had nothing to do with his arousal for her, which was primal and intense, but she'd never given him a second chance. Had barely ever given him even a second glance since that shitty night.

He needed to prove to Nicole—and to himself—that he was worthy of her time. Worthy, if he was lucky, of a place in her bed. At least for a little while.

Somehow, he would find a way to show her, finally, that he wasn't the waste of space she thought he was. Maybe it would take a supernatural effort, but he'd do it. He'd find a way. Thoughts of lust potions had him feeling all inspired and mystical. And horny as hell.

Nicole, his fantasy in blue—here he came. Armed with the lust potion of the gods, no less.

2

"YOU CAN'T POSSIBLY BELIEVE that's some kind of love potion."

Nicole Arroyo had heard a lot of bullshit in the three years since she'd made detective, but a magic love potion just about took the biggest-load-of-crap award. If the man standing next to her desk had been anyone else, she might have reacted with a little more diplomacy.

"Not love potion," Ethan said. "*Lust* potion."

Nicole didn't suffer fools or devil-may-care Englishmen. Especially not when the Englishman went by the name Ethan Ramsey and had a bad habit of popping in on her unwelcome whenever he stopped by the precinct on one of his relentless information-gathering excursions. He may have been a tirelessly devoted journalist, but something about him bugged her, made her feel off-balance and a little too... impassioned, or something.

The very fact that he could show up with something he claimed was a lust potion and she wasn't laughing her ass off at him told her all she needed to know about how off-kilter he made her feel. She stared at the bottle in his hand, knowing without even considering its contents that it was fake, and that Ethan knew it was fake, too, but was there with the stuff just to screw with her.

He was one of those guys she could tell spent a lot of time dancing around his bedroom in a pair of bikini briefs. He probably didn't even need music.

And his dark brown hair, the way it was ever so slightly in disarray—*pulleaze*. His appearance was always so carefully casual, so appealing yet a tad mussed, she knew he had to have worked hard to attain it. He clearly thought too much about the way he looked and was way too pleased with himself for being so absurdly attractive. How could a human being even have such impossibly blue eyes? He probably wore colored contacts.

But, okay, she had to admit, what pissed her off the most about Ethan was not that he tried so hard to look hot, but that she fell for it. And so did other women. Wherever he went, women practically stripped off their panties in response to his walking into a room.

Nicole would not ever again be one of those fools.

"And where, exactly, did you find this lust potion?"

"A little tourist shop called Jag's at the edge of the Gaslamp Quarter," he said, tilting the bottle to and fro. "Damn it, the bottle's leaking."

He wiped his hand on his pants, then checked the cork to make sure it was on securely.

"So you bought a bottle of so-called *lust* potion, and you're only now realizing maybe you were ripped off?"

"I didn't buy it. The shopkeeper planted it on my friend."

"Planted it?"

"Yep, as in, stuck it in her purse when she wasn't looking. The police were headed into the shop when it happened."

"So he was possibly trying to get rid of evidence," Nicole said, eyeing the bottle with newfound interest.

"That's my guess," he said, but his voice sounded far away. "I was on my way to turn it over to the lab, but— Oh, bloody hell, this stuff is still leaking everywhere."

She snapped back to attention. He held up his hand and sniffed it.

"Doesn't smell like anything. Do you have a tissue or something I could wipe this off with?" he asked.

"Right over there," she said, nodding at the bookshelf against the wall with the tissue box on top.

"Hey, before I clean this off, why don't we do a little experiment—you know, see if it works?"

Nicole laughed. "You be my guest and take a drink of it."

"That's the thing. I'm not sure if you're supposed to drink it, or…" He closed the distance between them, rounding her desk, entering her space.

Her carefully guarded space.

"Go ahead, take a whiff," Ethan said, holding his hand out.

"Let me get this straight—you want me to sniff your hand?"

He flashed his signature smile, and somewhere out there, a woman's panties spontaneously combusted.

"This is ridiculous."

"Come on. Just one little whiff."

His hand was a few inches from her nose now, and the only way she could think to get rid of it was to smell it and shut him up. One sniff could put to rest for good the possibility that some exotic lust potion was on the loose in San Diego.

She edged her nose closer by an inch and inhaled deeply. He was right—there was no scent, save that of Ethan. That warm, almost-woodsy scent that lingered in her mind, even after two years and no satisfaction.

But then a white flash blinded Nicole for a split second, and a crazy-hot image flashed in her mind. Bare limbs intertwined, a woman's hand against the naked flesh of a man's back, a woman's legs wrapped around a man's narrow hips—and then their faces, rapt with pleasure.

It was her and Ethan.

Her breath caught in her throat for a moment, but she recovered, took a step back and bumped into her bookshelves.

She shook the image out of her head, but a sudden warming trend started in her neck and moved south, turning into a full-fledged electrical storm when it reached its destination between her thighs.

She looked up at him and their gazes locked. He was staring at her as if he'd been hypnotized, and now she had a vague sense she was doing the same to him. She felt herself moving forward, felt a burst of pure pleasure as Ethan came closer.

Closer, and closer still. A magnetic force pulled them together, and there was no fighting it.

Nicole felt as if she were seeing him—really seeing him—for the first time, and she couldn't imagine why she'd been able to mostly resist him until now.

He was irresistible.

And then her mouth was against his, and they were locked in a desperate kiss that was all tongues and lips. All grasping and wanting.

It was strange how she had no actual recollection of deciding to press her body against Ethan's, twine her arms around him, and kiss him.

She was only aware of the here and now. Only cognizant of the rough heat of his kiss, the texture of his lips, the urgent pressure of his hands against her neck, against her waist.

She heard a moan and realized it was coming from her. She was moaning into his mouth. Her leg snaked around Ethan's as her appetite for him took on epic proportions. She wanted him with a fierceness she'd never felt before, and she wanted him right now.

How had they gotten here to this delicious place, and how would she ever let go?

And was that actually her hand now traveling down his shoulder, over his chest, to his waist, and below?

When she felt the solidness of his erection, she couldn't doubt the reality of their embrace any longer. The warm pleasure coursing through her nearly drowned out the voice of protest about where her hand was and where they were at that very moment.

In her office…at the precinct…anyone could see.

Horribly…ridiculously…unprofessional.

Nicole felt them moving dangerously toward a destination the small voice in her head now cried out that she didn't want to go. She struggled out of the deep fog that had overtaken her, and she untwined her arms and leg from Ethan and willed herself to push him away.

Her lips weren't obeying. She continued to kiss him. But no. They couldn't go any further than this.

Been there, done that…no going there again.

Must…stop…now.

With every ounce of her strength, she forced herself to break away from the kiss.

"No, we can't do that," she said. But her voice didn't sound very convincing.

Ethan gazed at her through what looked like a fog of his own, barely comprehending her puny protest.

She took a step back from him, then another step, instinct telling her that putting some distance between them was her only hope. She bumped up against the bookcase again, then scrambled sideways, farther away.

"What's the matter?" he asked, breathless.

"This! We can't do this," she said, more determined now.

With a few feet between them, the fog in her brain wasn't so thick now, and she could hear the warning voice a little louder. It was saying, *Stay the hell away from him. Stay the hell away!*

Ethan blinked at her as if she'd just spoken to him in Urdu.

"Ethan? Are you okay?"

Stupid question. He was clearly anything but okay.

He stepped toward her again. "I want you, Nicole. And you want me." Another step closer, and Nicole felt that crazy buzzing again. "Why do we have to fight it?"

She grabbed the rolling desk chair next to her and pushed it between them, holding on to the back of it ready to slam it into his shins if he came any closer.

"Listen to me," Nicole said. "That stuff, whatever the hell it is—it's affecting our brains. Maybe it's some kind of odorless inhalant drug."

"You can't blame this thing between us on a fake lust potion. The attraction's been there since long before today."

She held out her hand. "Give that bottle to me, and

I'll turn it over to the lab for analysis. You may be in possession of an illegal substance."

"Are you going to charge me and book me?" he said. "Maybe handcuff me and drag me off to a private room where you can—"

"Stop it. You know there's something freaky going on here."

She glanced over at the open door into the office, horrified at the thought that one of her co-workers might have caught the lurid sight of herself and Ethan engaged in mutual tonsil inspection a minute ago. No one was nearby. Thank God.

"What's weird is that we can have a kiss like that, and you can act like it wasn't supposed to happen."

Another step closer, and Nicole's will to resist him nearly vanished again. She pushed the chair as hard as she could toward him and it glanced off his shins. Then she climbed on her desk and slid across, knocking papers and files on the floor as she went, swinging her legs over on the other side. She kept moving until she reached the doorway.

"Leave that stuff on the desk, and get the hell out of here."

Ethan seemed to want to speak, but he said nothing. Instead, he dutifully set the bottle down and came toward the door. Nicole edged backward the closer he came, and when he passed her, she took another big step away just to be safe.

Out in the main office, they garnered a few curious glances, but nothing more. She stood in her office doorway and watched as Ethan slowly made his way across the room to the hallway, glancing over his shoulder every few seconds as if he wanted to come running back. He looked like a man entrusting a bag of gold to a stranger, not quite sure if he really should.

And Nicole, even with the fog drifting out of her head, wanted to stop him so badly she could feel his name on the tip of her tongue, and it took every ounce of her willpower not to say it.

She was so damn predictable.

Nicole couldn't help loving men. It was in her genetic makeup. Every Arroyo woman for as far back as she knew had harbored a legendary weakness for the male gender, and each and every one of them—except Nicole—had the train-wreck love lives to prove it.

It was one thing to like men, to enjoy their company, to think they were a useful addition to the human race. It was quite another to have the soul-deep lust for them that the Arroyo women had. Nicole could spend a lifetime studying the lines of a man's body, savoring the hot, musky scent of male flesh, losing herself in the way he felt on her, inside her, against her.

She had a bad habit of losing herself to men, and she knew it all too well. So as a grown-up woman, she'd made the very conscious choice to stay away from the kind of men who made her get lost. She dated the safe ones instead.

Safe, as in domesticated. Never those wild, untamed men who ignited primal urges in her. But always the men who were polite, not too demanding…and never too passionate. These men she could remain in control with, and she always knew there'd be no danger of unleashing the passion that couldn't be contained.

She wasn't sure which category Ethan Ramsey fell into. On the one hand, he'd proven himself to be a lackluster lover on that one disastrous night two years ago when job stress and pent-up lust had led to her giving in to his flirtation. But on the other hand, he'd been drunk, and she'd felt wildly turned-on by him before things had fizzled out. She'd sensed that beneath his laid-back exterior lurked a man of great passion.

That night she'd bumped into him at a trendy pub she'd never been to before—and hadn't been to since—and already knowing him from his coverage of a few cases she'd worked on, she'd thought he would be a safe one-night stand.

Instead, she'd gotten another lesson in why it was always a bad thing to lose control.

She turned and eyed the bottle Ethan had left behind. What the hell was that stuff? Or was it simply all her long-ignored libido that was to blame for the scorching kiss?

"Hey, Arroyo," a male voice said, jarring her out of her thoughts.

Nicole turned around to find Tom Yates, the office clerk, standing next to her. "What's up?" she said.

"I just heard Jonas Pulatski's made parole. Thought you'd want to know."

Dear God.

Just the freaking news she needed. Her stomach twisted at the horrible memories that name dredged up. She'd known he was up for parole, and she'd blocked out the painful fact from her mind.

Jonas and his sixteen-year-old little brother Carl had been involved in an armed robbery at a convenience store. Nicole and her partner Max Robbins had been called to the scene. She hadn't made detective yet—had only been on the street for six months. Carl had panicked when the police showed up, shot at her, and Nicole had returned fire, killing him. He was the first and last man—no, *child*—she'd ever killed. Jonas, a longtime street thug, had killed Max.

Jonas had sworn revenge on Nicole before going to prison, but he must have learned to keep his mouth shut about such things while serving his time, hence the parole.

"Thanks for letting me know," she said.

"You look a little pale. Are you okay?"

"Sure," she said and went to get the bottle of mystery potion to take to the lab.

She needed to get the hell out of here, like *now*. And since she needed to know what was in the bottle, it was the best excuse she could think of to get away from her office.

As if she didn't have enough to worry about with Jonas Pulatski being on the loose, she also had that kiss to dwell on. That impossible, fiery kiss that had made her want to throw Ethan onto the nearest horizontal surface and ride him like a wild stallion.

A wave of heat washed over her again, and she sat down with a thump on the edge of her desk, steadying herself. What the hell was going on?

Had that fake lust potion contained some kind of toxic chemical that was screwing with her brain?

Could she trust herself to walk through the building to the lab without embarrassing herself any further? What if Ethan wasn't gone yet? What if he was still standing around talking to someone?

If her co-workers saw her getting all hot and bothered by some guy—a reporter, no less—they'd never let her live it down. Nicole couldn't say she loved the male-dominant culture in the police department, but she did love her job.

She loved being part of the thin blue line that stood between civilization and chaos, and she wouldn't do anything to jeopardize her career. Even if it meant pretending she wasn't a real woman with real physical needs whenever her colleagues were around.

But today, all of a sudden, she was feeling as if her physical needs could absolutely not be ignored—or controlled.

3

ETHAN FORCED HIMSELF to walk away. It was the most arduous walk of his life, leaving Nicole there, their personal business unfinished.

How to explain what had happened? Was there any rational explanation for a kiss that had felt as if it was burning the soles off his shoes?

Maybe it was just her. After all, whenever Ethan could make up an excuse to put himself in Nicole's vicinity, he became possessed with fantasies about him, her, and the handcuffs she surely had stashed in her purse. It was a fruitless pursuit, since he stood little chance of finding himself in the territory that included her panties again in this lifetime.

Still, she fascinated him. She tried really hard to look like a professional. She pulled her long dark hair back into a severe bun at her nape, but this only drew attention to the delicate satin flesh of her neck, skin, he knew, that was as ripe and delicious as a summer peach.

She also tried to hide her curves behind an array of restraining undergarments. Ethan had encountered several of them on his one and only night with Nicole, and if he hadn't been so damn drunk, he might not have found the heavy-duty bra and girdle such a challenge. But a few too many pints of Guinness and the late night led to an embarrassing fumbling attempt at passion that had ended with him passing out and her disappearing from the hotel room before dawn, never to grace his presence again.

At least not voluntarily. He found reasons to stop by her desk at the precinct whenever he could, usually under the guise of work. Each encounter, however brief, fueled his pathetic fantasies. Sure, he could have other women, but there was something about Nicole.

Something smoldering, burning just below the surface. All her tightly wound control—the facade she presented to the world—concealed a wild, passionate woman. He just knew it. He'd seen a glimpse of that woman and he longed to fully unleash her.

No, *unleash* was the wrong word. It made him think of large snakes trapped in burlap sacks. Wrong image entirely. Maybe unravel was the right word. Or, simply, undress.

God knew he'd had a never-ending succession of fantasies about the ways in which he wanted to undress her, strip her bare, and take his own sweet time about exploring every lush spot on her body. Kissing, licking, tasting, burying his face in her flesh and drinking her in like water.

Sure, maybe it was a bit of his hidden control freak nature coming out in his wanting Nicole so much. He wanted her partly because he couldn't have her. While the rest of the world might not have been aware of the type-A personality lurking beneath his easygoing exterior, Ethan couldn't deny its presence. He liked to feel in control of his world, and Nicole was utterly and completely out of his control. That unfortunate night—or more accurately, his failure to perform— were perfect examples of the effect she had on him.

Ethan would not—could not—let this latest encounter with Nicole end in one hot, incredibly frustrated kiss.

So what? What else could he do?

And why did his brain feel so damn fuzzy and sluggish?

Well, not sluggish exactly, but…maybe dazed was a better word. He felt as if he were waking up from a long, ill-timed sleep—the kind he always ended up having after suffering jet lag from the eight-hour time difference between London and San Diego.

Maybe Nicole had been right about the lust potion having some sort of narcotic effect. Or maybe…

Maybe it really had been a lust potion the lizard man had planted on Zoe. It wasn't outside the realm of his imagination that the right combination of chemicals could produce a high level of arousal. Especially if the people involved already had some latent—or in Ethan's case, blatant—attraction to each other.

He wandered to the main desk of the police station and asked the clerk which officer on duty could answer his questions about the multiple homicide case he was researching. Twenty minutes later, he'd gotten everything he needed to complete his story, and had no further excuse to linger there any longer.

On his way back to the car, his mobile phone rang, and he saw Zoe Aberdeen's number appear on the LCD.

"What's up?" he answered.

"Did you turn in that love potion crap to the crime lab?"

"Just now dropped it off, actually."

"Oh good. I was a little worried you'd decide to keep it, and I just have kind of a weird feeling about that stuff."

Should he tell her about the odd effect the stuff had had on himself and Nicole?

His brain answered immediately with a resounding "Hell no." Not only would such a claim make him sound as if he'd gone dotty, but he didn't exactly have any facts to back up the story, either.

No, the whole lust potion thing had to stay top secret if he hoped to avoid becoming the laughingstock of the news office.

"So you seemed a little distracted or something at lunch today. Anything going on that I should know about?"

"Are you that hard up for gossip that you're dredging up dirt on my personal life?"

Zoe was the *Times's* gossip columnist, and therefore a notoriously bad person to spill, say, the details of one's short-term dalliances with local celebrities.

"Hardly. I just worry about you. You don't seem to be your usual jovial self is all."

"Did Kathryn put you up to this?"

"No—well, maybe a little. She knows I'm the pro at digging up dirt, and she noticed your strange mood, too. We were just talking about how distant you'd seemed over lunch."

"I'm not sure what to say. I guess maybe I could have been a little distracted thinking about the story I've been working on, but that's all," Ethan said as he unlocked his car and got in.

He put his key in the ignition, started the engine, and put the car in Neutral.

"Let's be honest here. We're pretty sure you're not a born-again virgin, but lately, you've made no mention of your social life. You used to tell us all about your exploits."

"Um, no, actually I never told you more than the most public details. Besides, what do you care if I've decided to stop whoring around?"

Ethan hadn't even realized it before Zoe's comment, but she was onto something. Lately he really had let his social life die down, and he'd been throwing himself into his work more and more. He had no idea why, except maybe it was the one area of his life that he was sure had any meaning.

"I'm nosy, and we're worried about you. Any un-attached thirty-year-old male is subject to speculation in these harsh dating times."

"I see," he said, but he didn't. "Were you hoping to remedy my problem? Perhaps make some more dreadful matchmaking efforts on my behalf?"

"Liza Wittaker was not dreadful, and neither was—"

"Oh, you know what I mean. I know how you and Kathryn are, always thinking you have the perfect friend for me to hook up with."

"We just love you, Ethan. Not that either of us are even remotely attracted to you—"

"Of course not," he said wryly.

Zoe laughed. "Because we know what a pain in the ass it would be to always have to fend off all the other women who are attracted to you."

"I like that story much better. Let's go with that one."

"It's true. So, let's hear the details. What's up with your vacant social calendar?"

"It's just a little dry spell, but I like how you buttered me up with flattery before zeroing back in on your information-gathering mission."

"Please don't tell me you've slept with and pissed off every available female in San Diego."

"It's true. I'll be moving on to Orange County

next. The commute will be hell, but I hear the girls there are easier."

Zoe's snort of laughter drowned out the sound of Ethan's car stereo for a moment. "Are you ever serious?"

"I try to avoid it. Morose is a bad look for me. I don't want to get frown lines, and I can't afford bi-monthly Botox."

"Oh God, speaking of Botox, you'll never guess who's getting it...."

Ethan didn't hear anything else Zoe said, because Nicole suddenly exited the building. She walked to her car, her lush ass a sight for sore eyes in a pair of navy blue pants.

He could almost feel the dense fog settling on his brain again, and he wondered for a moment if it would be safe to drive in such a state. But there was little time to consider such matters, because he knew without thinking about it that he would follow her.

"Listen, Zoe? I've gotta go. We'll chat later, okay?"

Zoe said something about him not getting away with excuses about dry spells, but he hung up the phone before she could get too far on the rant.

Why the hell did he want to follow Nicole so badly, anyway? He didn't go chasing after women for no apparent reason. But maybe if he confronted her once and for all, and aired out the issues about that night two years ago, they'd have a chance of moving forward with a clean slate. Perhaps a chance to explore the very real attraction he knew there was between them.

It was as if some magnetic force was keeping him within orbit of her. As if he faced a vicious hurtling into outer space if he dared let her out of his sight.

She was a cop though—detective no less—and it wasn't as if he could hope to tail her without being noticed. To minimize the risk of being spotted, he kept a safe distance behind her car, and when he saw that she was headed in the direction of her apartment, he followed without worry about staying close. He knew where she lived, and even if she didn't go straight there, she'd end up there eventually.

Twenty minutes later, he pulled into an empty spot across the street from her apartment. Her car was already parked, and she was nowhere in sight—presumably already in her apartment.

So now what? He couldn't exactly pound on her door and demand another kiss. But he couldn't drive away either. All he knew was that he had to stay close to her, had to find another opportunity to talk to her, and he hoped, pick up where they'd left off.

His stomach growled, but he felt no hunger. He hadn't eaten anything since lunch, and it was dinnertime now. Normally he'd be ravenous. Instead, his entire being was focused on Nicole as if she was his only hope for nourishment.

He thought again of the lust potion—wondered

what, exactly, it might have done to him. Was he going to grow hairy palms and weird skin patches? Was he going to starve to death following Nicole around at a safe distance for the next week? Or would she put him out of his misery and shoot him before then?

Safe distance, hell. Without really deciding to do it, Ethan suddenly knew that he would get out of the car and go take a peek in Nicole's window.

Just a quick peek.

How that would give him a chance to talk to her, he couldn't say. Shouldn't he have been walking up to her door and knocking on it? No, he needed a chance to compose his thoughts first before he aired all the stuff that always went unspoken between them.

He was possessed with the idea of seeing her, knowing what she was doing at this very moment. He could barely remember getting out of the car, crossing the street, or rounding the building.

If he recalled correctly from having tracked her down to apologize after their disastrous night together, she lived in the left corner apartment. As he stared up at her balcony, he realized the second-floor location might be a problem, but the apartment below hers had a conveniently placed picnic table on the patio, and surely the resident wouldn't mind if he used it to get a foot up.

He tugged the table out a bit, then climbed onto it, got a hold onto the wrought-iron rails of the balcony, and tested his weight. He tried to stay fit, but he'd never before needed to access a second-story balcony without the aid of stairs, and it was only occurring to him as he swung a leg up onto the edge of the balcony that he was demonstrating a surprising amount of strength for a guy who spent most of his day tapping away at a computer. He pulled himself all the way up without breaking a sweat and found himself on Nicole's rather desolate-looking balcony. A lone beach chair sat neglected, a layer of dust muting its blue and purple stripes.

The blinds for the sliding glass doors to the balcony were partly open, and Ethan could see into Nicole's living room.

Lamplight illuminated the room, but there was no one in sight. Nicole's purse and a stack of mail lay on the small dining room table that sat between the living room and the galley kitchen.

So now what? Press his nose to the window and wait? Had he lost his freaking mind?

Quite possibly.

Some small nagging voice in his head said this was absurd—climbing onto balconies and lurking at a woman's window. A woman cop, no less, who would not hesitate to shoot him if she thought he harbored ill intent.

But some baser force propelled him forward. Possessed him with the desire to see Nicole, to be close to her, to have her naked body against his—

Ethan threw himself against the edge of the

balcony when Nicole appeared in the hallway wearing nothing but a pair of panties and a bra. He flattened himself, hoping the six inches of wall concealed him from her view.

"Bloody hell," he muttered under his breath, his heart thudding maniacally in his ears.

She'd know for sure that he was an irredeemable freak if she found him loitering out here. Not exactly the image that makes a woman want to hop into bed with a man.

When, after a few moments, there were no screams or gunshots, he eased his head forward until he could see into the living room again. Nicole stood with her back to the patio door—her glorious satin back—as she read through her mail. His gaze dropped immediately to her ass, bared by a black lace thong instead of the granny girdle he'd encountered that night. Round, full and firm, it was the kind of ass a man dreamed of grabbing onto and holding tight, the kind of ass rappers wrote songs about.

His cock stood up in his pants, and he looked down stupidly at himself. Now he really was officially a pervert, standing on a woman's balcony with a hard-on.

But then he noticed for the first time that he'd ripped the knee of his pants somehow. Must have happened while climbing onto the balcony. His knee had been cut, too, and was bleeding, but he hadn't even felt it. Even now, upon seeing the wound, he barely felt the sting of it.

This whole day was getting weirder by the minute, with no end to the weirdness in sight. He couldn't even recognize his normal, responsible, non-crazed self right now.

Nicole moved, catching his attention again, and he watched in utter appreciation of her body and the way she moved as she walked across the room toward the kitchen. She picked up a phone, dialed a number, and paced back and forth as she waited on the line. Ethan strained to hear her as she spoke…something about going out, dinner, a nightclub called La Casa, a girl named Serena's inability to resist some guy named Rick…

He lost the sound of her voice as she left the room and went down the hallway.

Ethan leaned back against the wall again and closed his eyes, wondering not for the first time what the hell he was doing and what crazy force had taken him in a matter of hours from being a sane and rational reporter to being a peeping tom with a boner trespassing on a balcony.

A peeping tom with degrees from both Oxford and Stanford. A well-educated pervert, so to speak. He could amuse himself by reciting Proust and Milton as he whiled away his years in prison. The parole board probably wouldn't look kindly on a man who'd been sexually harassing a police officer when he was arrested.

And being English wouldn't exactly make him the most intimidating inmate on the cell block. Some big bastard named Bubba would probably think his accent sounded pretty and decide to make him his bitch, and then Ethan would be screwed in a whole new way. Quite literally.

Did he really want Nicole to the point of lunacy simply because he couldn't have her? Was that what this was all about? Or was there something more...? Maybe. Sure she interested him in profound ways, but he'd never pursued a woman who'd made it clear she didn't want to be pursued. Not only was he so not one of those can't-take-no-for-an-answer guys, but he'd always had enough women pursue *him* that he didn't need to chase one who didn't want him.

He'd always prided himself on being a great lover. Not an adequate one, not a prolific one. A *great* one. Great lovers didn't leave their women unsatisfied. Great lovers made up for unfortunate incidents. That had to be the reason he couldn't let Nicole go.

He probably should have dismissed all that wounded pride garbage, but being here on Nicole's balcony had little to do with that. Whatever had driven him here was beyond his comprehension and nearly beyond his control.

It was some kind of lust gone wild, he feared.

"Hey! What the hell are you doing up there?" Ethan heard a woman's voice call out from below.

His heart nearly sprang out of his mouth as he turned toward the sound and spotted a tiny African-American woman wearing a leopard-print satin robe. Her arms were crossed over her chest, and her glare nearly shot fire.

"I said, what the hell are you doing up there? Don't you know a cop lives there? She'll shoot your ass if she catches you—"

Ethan plastered on his most innocent expression and held a finger up to his lips to silence the woman.

"Don't you go shushing me, you mother—"

"Please," he tried to say just loud enough for the woman to hear, "I'm trying to surprise my girlfriend. It's her birthday, and…she's inside looking for clues I planted for her to find me out here."

"Uh-huh. If you were her boyfriend planting clues in her apartment, why haven't I seen you here before, and why'd you have to use my table to get up there? Don't you have a key?"

"Please, ma'am. Don't spoil the surprise. I'll explain later, okay?"

He was going to prison. Straight to San Quentin with the guy named Bubba and the lifelong Proust recitations.

"I'm about to march my ass upstairs and knock on your so-called girlfriend's door to let her know she's got some crazy bastard on her balcony—and you better stay the hell off my picnic table, you hear?"

She said all that in about five seconds without taking a breath.

Ethan opened his mouth to protest, but the woman was gone in a flash. He looked left and right, calculating his best escape route. A glance at Nicole's living room, which was still free of her, gave him some hope that he wouldn't be discovered.

He'd just determined that his best bet for escaping without a broken limb was to risk the neighbor's wrath and jump down onto the picnic table again when she reappeared armed with a cordless phone and a baseball bat.

"Ma'am, just let me explain," he said.

"Yeah, you explain to that cop whose balcony you're trespassing on," she said. "I'm calling her right now."

It was now or never. While she was distracted by the phone call, he had to pray her aim with the bat would be a little off.

Ethan swung himself over the balcony railing, lowered himself, and right before he jumped down, he caught sight of Nicole reentering the living room, the phone still pressed to her ear.

"Damn busy signal," the woman said down below.

The sight of Nicole's large, full breasts encased in black lace nearly halted him in his escape, and he felt that sense of euphoria descending on him once more. His cock stirred in his pants again—for God's sake, did it have no shame?—and his whole body seemed to hone in on Nicole and her glorious, perfect mounds of flesh.

"You bastard!" the neighbor was saying now. "You better be glad your so-called girlfriend doesn't have call waiting."

He'd hesitated for a moment too long, and now he'd probably have his head bashed in with a Louisville Slugger, just for an extra glimpse of some very nice breasts.

The moment his feet touched the picnic table, he felt the hard thud of the baseball bat against his thigh. He expelled a curse. The pain took a while to register, as he scrambled off the table and away from the crazed woman. But she followed and swung again, this time making contact with his shoulder.

And now the dull ache in his leg was nothing compared to the bone-deep pain in his shoulder. Still, it felt duller than a high-velocity pounding with a baseball bat should have…as if his body had some newfound tolerance for pain.

"You better get your sorry white ass back here!"

Ethan kept running, figuring it wouldn't do any good to defend his motives now, not when he was unarmed. He rounded the building with the woman still chasing him, then had to fear for the life of his car when he realized she'd probably catch up before he managed to pull away.

He ran for all he was worth, scrambled into his

BMW, locked the doors, started the engine and was just pulling away when he heard the bash of the bat against the rear of his car.

"Damn it!" he cursed at the steering wheel, burning rubber as he left the scene.

Knowing his luck, she was memorizing his license plate number right now.

Thank God Nicole didn't know what kind of car he drove. And thank God she didn't have call waiting. And thank God the neighbor hadn't thought to call 911 instead of the cop living upstairs from her. But what if the neighbor did memorize his plate number, and she did give it to the police? He glanced into his rearview mirror and saw her looking at something on the bottom of her shoe, rather than studying his plates, and heaved a small sigh of relief. It appeared he'd dodged that one little swing of the bat.

But, he realized, as he rounded the corner toward the freeway, what bothered him most wasn't his beating, or the car's beating. What really had him freaking out was that he was driving farther and farther away from Nicole.

4

NICOLE COULDN'T STOP thinking about sex. She'd driven home from work all distracted, her insides doing that crazy buzzing thing the entire way.

She'd gotten herself ready for girls' night out in a state of half arousal, suffered through dinner with her friends the same way, and now that they were at their favorite Friday night hangout, La Casa, she wasn't in much better shape.

She was not a woman who did one-night stands—except for that one not-so-notable exception. She didn't even do third or fourth date sex. She never slept with a guy until their relationship was guaranteed exclusive and straight-up protected by condoms, birth control pills and preferably a clearance from the doctor that the guy was clean. By her friends' standards, she was a good girl, a prude, a total drag when it came to sex.

But that was only because she knew what she was capable of. Within her lurked a woman who could too easily get out of control. She was determined to keep that part of herself in check or wear out her vibrator trying.

Thanks to her mother, her aunts and her sisters, she'd seen firsthand what happened to women who were too passionate and too spontaneous. They all loved men too much—always the wrong men—and they all had the thwarted dreams to prove it.

Ever since Nicole had been a little girl drooling over Johnny Depp on *21 Jump Street,* she'd known she wanted to be a police officer. Maybe it had been stupid to look to TV for her role models, but that was about the only place she'd seen women who hadn't had their lives bogged down by no-good men and accidental pregnancies. None of the women on TV looked tired all the time or lived in run-down trailer parks. Nicole had fiercely wanted to be one of those in-control women, and now she was.

She would never, ever let anything jeopardize that.

There had only been one night when she'd broken all her rules. With Ethan.

"Something is seriously wrong with me."

Nicole surveyed her companions at the small round table—the Reality Check Sisters, as she liked to call them. They were all staring back at her suspiciously, as if they sensed the dire nature of her situation.

"You look all tense like you just got finished with a smack-down on some scumbag. I don't like you dealing with all those criminals and lowlifes. It's not safe."

This from Serena, a woman who'd survived two yearlong tours in Iraq as an army captain.

"I know what's wrong with you—you haven't gotten laid in, like, three months," Juliana said, piping in ever so helpfully.

"You've been counting?" Nicole asked, trying to do a quick mental calculation in her head.

There had been that couple of months with Randall, who lived on a boat—he'd been great, but she couldn't get over the whole motion sickness thing—and then…nothing…for three months apparently.

"I've just got a good head for numbers, that's all."

"She keeps tabs on everyone," Keilani said, rolling her eyes. "She wants to make sure no one's having more sex than her."

"A noble goal," said Juliana, "but—"

"But nothing! That has nada to do with what's wrong with me," Nicole blurted before she could think the position through.

Maybe though, on second thought, there was a connection.

"Okay," Serena said. "We're all ears."

The three women sipped their drinks simultaneously, waiting for Nicole to spill her story.

"There's this guy I used to have a bit of a crush on. Totally not my usual type, but we kind of had a one-night stand a few years back—"

"Kind of?" Keilani interrupted. "You? A one-night stand? Either you did or you didn't."

"Well, we did, but we *didn't*."

Three pairs of eyebrows arched suspiciously.

"Care to explain?" Serena said.

Nicole glanced around at the salsa club. This was about as safe a place as any to spill lurid details. The instrumental section of a song she didn't recognize was blaring, the dance floor was just starting to hop, and as soon as Nicole unloaded her problem, she was going to find a partner and dance up a good sweat.

La Casa, with its hip crowd of people who love to dance, was about as far from the preferred hangouts of Nicole's colleagues as she could get, and that suited her just fine. The last thing she needed was to run into a co-worker when she wanted to unwind and act like a real woman—not when she had to spend all her professional time pretending to be one of the guys.

"We tried to get down and dirty, but he couldn't get it up. Got it?"

A collective "Ooh" from her audience.

"I've got it—you *didn't* get it," Juliana said. "No wonder you're such a prude, if that's your sole experience with easy sex."

"Well, anyway, there was alcohol involved, and let's just say, I'm not willing to give him another chance. But I see him occasionally through work, and today I ran into him again, and it was like—bam, major chemistry all of a sudden."

"Why not give him another chance?" Keilani, queen of second chances, asked.

"Because he couldn't get it up the first time," Serena answered before Nicole could. Clearly an inexcusable offense in her book.

Nicole decided not to tell the whole truth, which was complicated and also would have involved divulging more details than she cared to divulge—that the "getting up" in question had actually happened, for a short while, and then sort of…fizzled out.

It had all been embarrassing and humiliating and totally not worth recounting in any great detail. But mainly it had been a relief, because she'd felt that detested uncontrollable passion surge with Ethan. Before the big letdown, she'd felt herself on the edge of becoming the kind of woman she'd always fought being.

"I have to see this guy around my office too much, for one thing. What if he tells someone at the precinct that we had a one-nighter?"

"What?" Serena said. "You're not allowed to have a sex life?"

"You know how it is—you were in the army. Everything we do is under more scrutiny."

"I know, I know, it just pisses me off."

"So anyway, I've been able to ignore him for two freaking years, and now all of a sudden, he walks into my office, and I can barely keep my hands off him."

"Sounds like you just need a surrogate dick. You know, to take the edge off." This from Juliana, who'd coined the *surrogate dick* phrase after her last boyfriend ditched her in the midst of what she claimed was the horniest time in her life. She'd managed to find stand-in penises aplenty to ease her frustration.

"And there's one fine prospect heading over here right now," Keilani said, nodding toward the bar.

Nicole oh so casually glanced in that direction and nearly dropped her bottle of Corona when she spotted Ethan, his gaze locked on her, his stride purposeful as he closed the distance between them.

"Oh, God," she whispered.

She sprang up from the table before he could reach her. "Excuse me," she said to her bewildered friends as she hurried toward Ethan. The last thing she needed was anyone getting a clue that he was the exact same guy she'd been talking about.

But a few feet away from him, that near-orgasmic sensation overtook her again, more intense now. She halted, gasping at the way her girl parts tingled.

This was *insane*.

He took a step closer, and there was no fighting the way she felt.

"How did you find me here?" she said, her voice coming out a little more breathy than she meant for it to.

He flashed a mischievous grin. "I'm a reporter, remember? I have my ways."

"You mean you followed me?"

"Not exactly."

"Why are you here?"

He was looking at her like he was a starving man and she was the last Big Mac on earth.

"Because, what happened in your office? It doesn't feel finished," he said, and oh, how she agreed with him.

"Yeah," she said.

"There's a lot of stuff between us we've never really talked about...." he said, then trailed off, his gaze growing more intense.

"It's all in the past," she said. "I only want to think about tonight."

She wanted to lick him—take all his clothes off and lick him up and down like a Popsicle.

But the last bit of reason left in her head said to get away from here. To get the hell away before she lost control again. She had to resist, and yet she couldn't muster the slightest bit of willpower to tell him to bug off.

And then there were her friends staring, and she had to play it cool. No licking, or arguing, or talking too much at all right now. No suspicious behavior. She glanced at the dance floor, the only place she could talk to Ethan at the moment—and hopefully find the will to tell him to get lost—without her friends being all over her with questions later.

"May I have this dance?" he asked, taking the hint.

"You know how to salsa?"

He shrugged, and his devil-may-care smile made an appearance. "A little. I might embarrass myself, but..."

Without thinking—or hesitating—Nicole took his hand and led him toward the dance floor, toward the safety of anonymous bodies and pulsing music. She needed him close—as close as possible.

She was seriously losing it.

"Then again, you might not," she said over her shoulder.

Amid the other dancers, they fell in step, their bodies molded against each other. Nicole told herself she was not supposed to enjoy herself. She was supposed to resist. Resist, resist, resist.

That's what her brain said, while her body just wanted to dance. To get closer. To feel and sweat and move.

He had good moves. Not very fancy ones, but good, solid moves.

"Where'd you learn this?" she asked, trying her damnedest now to think of anything but how incredible he felt against her and how badly she wanted to plunge her tongue into his mouth.

"I dated a dance instructor for a while. She taught me the basics."

"Lucky her," Nicole blurted, surprising even herself.

Her control was slipping more and more. She could feel it, but couldn't stop the momentum.

Ethan smiled slowly, probably realizing how far down her guard was.

She glanced over at her friends and caught them all staring with their mouths agape. She might as well have stripped off all her clothes and shimmied around on top of the bar naked, for the way they were looking at her. And then she looked down at herself and realized she and Ethan had nearly gone straight from hello to down-and-dirty bump-and-grind dancing of the sort that most people at La Casa didn't start doing until after midnight.

She had to stop, put her foot down, come to her senses and back the hell off. Somehow… But instead, she edged closer. She pulsed to the music, let it take control of her body, let their bodies intertwine as they danced.

No, she didn't let it happen. That wasn't quite accurate. Rather she felt herself watching it happen. She had already lost control.

Having him so close was like a drug. She inhaled his scent and felt dizzy with desire again. Too dizzy to dance. Too aroused to be here on a dance floor, with her friends' gazes following their every move. She may be horny, but she was no exhibitionist.

"Let's get out of here," she said, and before the words had finished forming on her lips, Ethan had her hand in his and was leading her off the floor, toward the door.

Somehow they made it to his car without stripping off any clothes. As he was unlocking the car, a glimmer of sanity appeared in her head. She thought of all her rules, all her strict avoidance of this kind of behavior. But she felt as though she was observing herself from above—too far away for any words of wisdom to be heard. So what if she let loose one more time?

What's the worst that could happen? A limp dick?

She could handle it. This time, she'd know what to do. She'd coax and tease and caress until she had him in a state of arousal so intense, there would be no turning back.

Somewhere between unlocking the car and climbing inside it, they'd started kissing, and thank God he had tinted windows in the rear, because now that they were in his backseat, articles of clothing had been tossed aside at lightning speed. Nicole was straddling Ethan, and when he took her breast into his mouth, she felt as if she'd come right then and there. Clasping the back of his head, she pushed him closer as he licked and teased, while her breath came out in ragged bursts.

He cupped her breasts in his hands as he kissed them, then he lifted and pushed them closer together so that he could move easily from one to the other and back again. Nicole arched her back, ground her pelvis against his erection, and felt a delicious burning between her legs more intense than she'd ever felt before.

No stopping now. She had to have him inside her, the sooner the better. She had to feel him filling her up and stretching her. Had to know if he was as good as he looked. As good as he tasted. As good as the intensity of their attraction promised.

His mouth moved up to her neck, then to her mouth,

where their hungry, urgent kisses left her raw. Their hands explored in a desperate frenzy, and their bodies moved against each other as if already making love. The only things standing between them were the fabric of her panties and his boxers, which she wanted to rip off at the seams.

"I want you," Ethan whispered, his voice low and husky.

"Do you have a condom?" she said, but he was already pulling one out of his wallet and taking the wrapper off.

"You're sure about this?" he asked, and for the first time, his glazed expression seemed almost lucid—almost free of their crazy desire.

"Shut up and do me," she said as she wrestled her way out of her panties.

Good thing he had a big backseat. She pushed him back on it, straddling him as he tugged aside his boxers and slid on the condom. He was hard now, fully aroused. Ready for her. And it felt in that moment like the sweetest sight she'd ever laid eyes on.

SOME PART OF ETHAN WANTED to take it slowly. He wanted to drive Nicole home, spread her out on a bed, and plunge his tongue inside her until she came in his mouth. Then he wanted to do it again. Then he'd lick every inch of her luscious body, memorize her every curve and dip. He'd let his hands take their time exploring her, let their bodies learn each other's rhythms, and then, when they could stand it no longer, he'd make love to her.

But that simply wasn't possible now.

A tsunami of desire had swept them out here into the car, into his backseat, and the only way it seemed he could save them was to plunge his cock inside her again and again until sanity returned.

But would it?

Ethan wanted to weep at the sight of Nicole straddling him in the cramped space, her breasts bobbing so close, her amazing honey-colored body like a work of art he could stare at all day. But there was this buzzing in his head, in his body, and the only way he could think to make it stop was to steady her hips, find her tight, wet opening, and push into her there.

He did, and she cried out in a sweet gasp of pleasure that echoed his own. He forced his way in as far as he could go, savoring how her body took him in, so tight, so hot.

"You feel like heaven," he whispered.

Her eyes were glazed over with pleasure, and she rocked her hips against him, bracing her hands on either side of his torso as best she could on the slanted leather seat, but he held her still to set his own rhythm with his feet braced against the floor and the door of the car.

He pounded against her, their bodies making a raw slapping sound, their breath coming out ragged and fierce. With each thrust he felt closer to some lifelong sought-after treasure. It was as if he'd found his purpose in life, to be inside this woman, here and now.

Her hips were soft and full, her pussy pliant but tight, and he could barely blink as he watched her face rapt with pleasure. She was a Mayan princess, exotic and beautiful beyond words. Her hair hung down thick and wavy over her shoulders—only the second time he'd ever seen it down. And her dark brown eyes, when she locked them on him, seemed so deep he could lose himself there.

And as he felt the delicious coiling inside of himself, the promise of release building up with such incredible tension that he could not imagine stopping it, he also had the fleeting thought that he'd found his soul mate in Nicole. Never mind that they barely knew each other, or that they were screwing like rabbits in the back of his car, or that she probably hated him. When he looked at her face, it was as if he was finding himself.

And then her release came, obliterating his crazy thoughts. Her body's contractions triggered his own orgasm, and they writhed against each other, all gasps and tangled limbs, desperate kisses and shuddering moans.

He came with such force he feared for a second that the condom might have shot off had it not fit so snugly. Nicole quaked against him, her breath heavy as it brushed his cheek. Then she buried her face in his neck and relaxed her body, his cock still inside her.

As he recovered from his orgasm, the fuzzy-headedness lifted from his brain for the first time since…since he'd been with Nicole at the precinct earlier…with the bottle of lust potion.

"Wow."

"Yeah, wow," she said.

"What the hell *was* that stuff?" he said.

"Hmm?" she murmured into his shoulder.

"That lust potion. Do you think maybe it could have been real?"

She laughed. Not something he'd witnessed often, and the sound of it was like hearing an old favorite song on the radio. He wrapped his arms around her and held her tight, recalling only now those crazy thoughts of love that had filled his head moments ago. Best not to mention that part, for sure.

"Do you believe in unicorns and fairies, too?" she asked.

"Only the magic ones," he said wryly. "Who knows. Maybe the potion does work. Or maybe that stuff just gave us an excuse to do what we've been wanting to do for years."

She was silent for a moment, and then, "Hmm. I don't know."

"Judging by what just happened," he said as he

looked her in the eyes, "we probably shouldn't let two years' worth of attraction bottle up inside us—"

His words were cut off by a sharp rapping at the windshield. "Police! Open up!"

He looked at Nicole, and she was looking at him with an expression that could only mean "Oh shit."

"Oh bloody hell," he muttered.

She scrambled off of him and was desperately tugging on items of clothing as he tried to pull his pants back up.

"Just a minute, officer!" she called out. "We're, um, changing clothes, that's all!"

A flashlight shone through the front window of the car, straight back at them, pinning Nicole in its beam. She halted with her top clutched over her chest, and Ethan understood in that moment how much more dire the situation was for her than for him.

"I'm sorry," he whispered. "I had no idea—"

"Sh!" She tugged on her top and shot him a glare that could halt criminals in their tracks. "Say as little as you can, and follow my lead."

5

NICOLE SHOULD HAVE KNOWN it would come to this. Her and Ethan, caught in the act, by one of her very own colleagues. A guy she'd chatted with at the precinct just last week, for God's sake. She felt blood warming her cheeks as the officer's flashlight spotlighted her face.

Nicole tugged her top all the way down and pushed the car door open, trying hard to act cool and calm. Not remotely embarrassed.

"Arroyo, is that you?" the officer, whose name tag read Hamlin, said as a look of confusion crossed his face.

Nicole still felt the slowed ability to think clearly, the heightened sense of Ethan's presence next to her. But she pushed it all aside as best she could and tried to think of a way out of this mess that wouldn't make her the laughingstock of the San Diego PD.

"Um, yeah, it's me," she said, her face burning.

Okay, there was probably no way to keep herself from being a laughingstock, but she could at least hope to salvage a shred of her pride.

She watched recognition dawn on the officer's face, and the answer became: probably not.

"I know this looks odd…." she said, at a loss.

Dear God, she'd lost the ability to think on her feet. And on her back. Something about Ethan had turned her into a mindless throbbing blob of sexual need.

Just freaking wonderful.

"You understand that what you were just doing qualifies as public indecency," the officer said, eyeing her, then Ethan, then her again for more emphasis, as if Ethan didn't really need to understand it, but she did.

And maybe that was true. In the stone ages.

"Absolutely. I used really poor judgment. I have to tell you, this was a stressful day at work, what with that Pulatski case coming back to haunt me. I just got carried away trying to unwind."

The officer's expression changed. Pulatski, a name that brought a grimace to every police officer's face. Jonas Pulatski shooting a cop as beloved as Max Robbins had hit everyone on the San Diego PD hard, especially Nicole.

"You worked on the Pulatski case?"

"I was the primary witness—the other cop on the scene the night Robbins was shot. He was my partner."

The officer made a pained expression. "I remember now. I'm sorry I didn't put two and two together."

Nicole hated using the Pulatski card, but maybe it was truer than she'd first imagined. Maybe that was the reason for her fuzzy thinking, her rash behavior, her carrying on like a woman with a death wish.

"We're very sorry, sir," Ethan chimed in.

She shot him a warning look, which he didn't catch.

"Is there any possible way you could, um, keep this quiet?" she asked.

The officer eyed her again. His expression was inscrutable, but she sensed his sympathy. "Sure. Just keep your stress relief in a private hotel room next time," he said, then looked at Ethan. "You know you got a busted taillight?"

"Oh that," Ethan said, sounding suddenly way too casual. "I just backed into my own mailbox today. I'll be sure to get it fixed right away."

Nicole looked over at the car and for the first time noticed that it was a black BMW. A black BMW with a busted taillight, just like the one her crazy downstairs neighbor had described earlier tonight. Nicole had just assumed her neighbor had stopped taking her medication again and was having delusions that she'd seen a man on Nicole's balcony, but now...

The officer nodded. "I'll let you off with a warning this time."

"Thank you so much," Nicole said. "Drop by my office any time you need a favor, okay?"

The officer nodded again and turned toward the club, then moved on. Nicole heaved a sigh of relief, and Ethan zipped up his pants.

"Wow, that was a close call," Ethan whispered.

"What the hell's the matter with us?" Nicole muttered as she got back in the car to see if there were any garments she'd left behind. Her bra hung from the headrest of the driver's seat. She grabbed it and looked around some more. Panties on the floor. She grabbed those too.

"I can hardly think of anything but doing what we just did—again," Ethan said.

"Slow down there, cowboy. You've proven your prowess." But she knew exactly what he meant. She was struggling to put those very thoughts out of her own head.

"It's not about that—it never has been. Well, maybe a wee bit."

"How'd you get that busted taillight?" Nicole asked, but she was having a hard time remembering now, with Ethan so temptingly close, why it mattered. Every other guy in the state of California drove around in a black BMW, so it wasn't exactly an uncommon car. Even if her neighbor hadn't been delusional, which she was.

"I really did back into my damn mailbox. Idiot thing to do, I know."

Sounded plausible. They were both sitting in the backseat again, and the quiet, the darkness, created a buffer from the world that made not touching Ethan nearly impossible. She wanted to reach out and trace her hand along his thigh, caress his cock, feel the hard ridges of his abs, absorb his warmth and his scent.

Her whole body ached for it. Again. Already.

What the hell was going on?

"You mention the Pulatski case and all of a sudden we're off the hook? Good deal."

Nicole exhaled, and it felt as if she was releasing demons from her body. "Long, miserable story. You've probably heard about it from the news—"

"Actually I'm familiar with Jonas Pulatski and his history. I interviewed him before his release from prison and am still researching a story I want to write about his crimes."

Her stomach lurched a little. "You? Interviewed Pulatski? Why?"

"It was something my editor mentioned wanting to do some in-depth coverage of, so I took on the task. I have to admit, knowing you made me more interested in the story overall, but I haven't wanted to dredge up painful memories for you by grilling you about it."

"That's pretty unusual for a reporter," Nicole said, surprised. Ethan had a reputation for being ruthless in his pursuit of the facts. "Thanks though. I appreciate your respecting my feelings about the subject."

"I can't take all the credit for being Mr. Sensitive. I was sort of waiting to see how much information I could get about the story without bothering you, before deciding if I'd ask you for an interview too."

She felt a little stab of betrayal, and she couldn't muster a response. Irrational, because what was he betraying?

"Would you be willing to talk about it later, if necessary?"

Nicole's throat closed up and refused to release any words.

"Bad question?"

"Very," she finally choked out. "I don't want to talk about it right now, okay? Too much baggage."

"Sorry, I didn't mean to pry."

"No, it's fine. It's just widely known that I'm not going to be all that well in the head what with Pulatski walking around free. That's why we were let go with a warning."

And Nicole wondered herself if she didn't need to take some vacation time or something. A little mental break from work-related stress, at least until she got used to the idea of Pulatski being on the outside. But that also felt like admitting failure somehow.

"So you think this thing with me and you, it's maybe stress-related?"

Nicole wanted that to be the truth. "Yes, definitely."

Maybe saying it would make it so.

She looked over at Ethan in the shadows of the backseat. His blue eyes always sparked as if he knew a dirty little secret that he was dying to tell, and his five-o'clock shadow just barely kept him from having the kind of baby face that made men look eternally young.

The thing that drove her craziest about him was that she could never tell if he was serious. Even now, he looked as if he was about to laugh. And okay, this *was* kind of funny, them getting caught in the act by one of her very own colleagues, but did he have to look that way right now, when they'd just been talking about the darkest time of her career?

Life was just a big cruel joke, and all he could do was laugh at it.

"I guess that doesn't explain why I still feel like I've gotten drunk on you and want more," he said.

"Why do you always look like you're about to laugh?"

He looked confused. "I do?"

"Yes, right now, you look like you're in on some secret joke."

He made a face. "I haven't a clue what you mean. I don't mean to make light of this, though it is kind of…bizarrely funny."

"See, right there. You just looked like you were going to laugh."

He shrugged. "I guess that's just my natural expression."

"Well, it's unnerving."

"I think the stress is going to your head a bit. Why don't I drive you home?"

"That'll be convenient for you, won't it?"

"I am hoping you'll invite me in for the night, if that's what you mean."

Nicole opened her mouth to protest, but the truth was, she didn't want to be alone tonight, and she desperately wanted to feel Ethan against her, inside her, again.

And easy as that, she decided.

"Okay," she said. "Come back to my place tonight, but I'm driving myself. I'm not leaving my car here."

"I'll follow you," he said, an odd expression crossing his face.

"Fine." She opened the door and got out, grabbed her purse from the floor of the car, dug around for her keys. "I'm parked two rows down," she said, pointing. "Left side, a white Honda Civic."

Nicole hurried to her car, her skin cold suddenly in the night air. Without Ethan's heat to warm her.

The more distance she put between them, the clearer her head was, the less overwhelmed by desire she was. But at the same time, she felt that magnetic pull in his direction. She wanted to turn and run back to him, fling herself in his arms, press her body against him.

The sex they'd just had was the most intense thing she'd ever experienced. Her body still tingled from the pleasure of it, and she still reeled from the reality of the whole thing.

Ethan most certainly had no worries about proving his manhood or his prowess or whatever. He was amazingly, profoundly, unbelievably good. Even in the backseat of his car.

She got in her Honda and started it, then pulled out when she saw Ethan waiting behind her. As she guided the car out of the lot and turned toward home, she allowed herself a moment to register just how far off the deep end she'd gone.

Careening off at full speed. And she still hadn't bothered to slam on the brakes, even as she was coasting midair toward the water.

It was so unlike her, she could hardly recognize her own actions. She felt as if she'd been possessed.

She *had* been possessed. By Ethan, of all people.

And now he was coming to her apartment.

He was going to spend the night and the idea excited her to no end. Made her press harder on the gas pedal until she was pushing the speed limit, until she was more than the five miles an hour over it she knew she could be without getting a ticket.

She needed a night like tonight. She didn't quite know why, and she wasn't going to question it. She needed it. And she needed it with Ethan. Tonight she would go wild, and she'd just have to worry about the consequences in the morning.

6

ETHAN WAS NOT GOING TO question his luck.

He knew how close he'd come to completely losing out on the rest of this night, and he wasn't going to take any risk—especially not getting arrested—that might screw it up.

He followed Nicole home in his car, possessed by that same aching need that had compelled him to climb onto her balcony and reinvent himself as a glorified stalker. He couldn't imagine letting her out of his sight. So he followed closely, aware all the time of her presence only a few car lengths away.

But what the hell else could he even do after that raging lust that had possessed them in the club and had swept them off into his backseat in a frenzy of nakedness and crazy desire? The sex they'd had was the most intense of his life, but also too short, and not nearly satisfying enough.

That was the thing about sex. It normally left one fully satisfied for a little while—at least fifteen minutes. And here he was feeling as if he hadn't yet gotten any satiation, as if instead of satisfaction, that amazing encounter had only left him needing more.

Was Nicole his addiction?

If so, why hadn't he felt it so strongly before?

Maybe there really was something to that potion, or maybe…maybe they were just incredibly overdue for this night.

In the morning, surely he'd feel satisfied.

They parked their cars in two spaces in front of Nicole's apartment building, and Ethan looked around for signs of the bat-wielding neighbor. He'd forgotten until the police officer mentioned it about his broken taillight, and he was surprised he'd managed to talk his way out of that little situation with Nicole. No, scratch that—not surprised. If she was as brain-fogged as he was, it was not so hard to believe she could dismiss the issue, even if her neighbor had alerted her to the fact that a guy in a BMW had been lurking outside her apartment.

The coast seemed to be clear, but he wondered belatedly if he should park somewhere else in the event the crazy woman recognized his car and beat it within an inch of its life. But if he tried to explain to Nicole why he couldn't park here, he'd have to admit to having been at her apartment already today. Which, well, could put a damper on the night, to say the least.

He took one look at her standing outside his car now, her skimpy skirt and top hugging her curves, and he decided to hell with the car.

Dangerous curves indeed.

He got out, locked the BMW, and followed her up the walkway to the building. She didn't speak, didn't even look back at him along the way. It was almost as if she was having second thoughts…or as if she wasn't sure what to say.

When they were inside her apartment, she switched on the light and dropped her purse on a table near the door.

"So this is the inner sanctum," Ethan said stupidly. As if he didn't already know what the place looked like from having peered through the balcony door earlier.

God, he was a freak.

Nicole kicked off her high heels and left them lying on the foyer floor, so he followed her lead and did the same. Maybe she was one of those people who didn't allow shoes in the house.

"I'm not much of a decorator," she said as if apologizing for something.

He looked around at bare white walls, a haphazard assortment of furniture, and a lonely-looking framed print of Gustav Klimt's *The Kiss* that hung on the wall over a tired black leather sofa. And he bit his lip to avoid making a joke. Definitely not the time for his warped humor.

"It's…nice."

"Oh shut up. It looks like a bad excuse for a bachelor pad."

"Well…"

She pulled off her top, and then pushed her skirt over her hips and let it drop to the floor. "There are other things I'm much more interested in than decorating."

Oh?

His mouth went dry, and whatever tiny bit of restraint he'd mustered vanished.

He had no recollection of closing the distance between them. There was only the feel of her flesh in his hands, the silken space where waist met hip, her tongue licking at his, their breath mingling, the hard resistance of the wall where he pinned her.

Hands fumbling to remove his clothes, extracting a condom for the ready, a gasp and a rush of pleasure as her hand found him and caressed.

He was lost in her and lost in the raging desire. Light cast across her bare breasts took his breath away for a moment, and he felt himself growing dizzy. He bent and kissed her there where light met flesh, tasted the salt from her perspiration after dancing in the hot nightclub, plunged his hand between her legs and found her wet with desire.

Ethan dropped to his knees, licked her, buried his tongue in her, licking and sucking and savoring her. He looked up at her, looking down at him, and his cock throbbed with the desire to be inside her. He'd never had a woman put him off as long as Nicole had, and her power to do that had also given her an incredible power to arouse him. No, actually, she'd always had the power to arouse him as no other woman could, but having her now after so long not having her was dizzying.

He felt both weak and unstoppable at the same time.

He felt as if he could move mountains with his dick, she aroused him so.

The sensation was almost like feeling in control, but not quite. He desperately wanted to have some control over the situation, some sense that he could have a say over his destiny where Nicole was concerned, but he feared a greater force was calling the shots here. And for now, he was willing to let himself go with that uncontrollable force if it meant having Nicole.

He pushed his tongue farther into her, savoring the sweet, musky taste, savoring the slippery wet feeling against his mouth, as her juices dampened his face. He coaxed her further and further until she squirmed her hips out of his grasp and grabbed him by the hair to pull him back up to her.

Then she dropped down herself, slowly, her gaze locked on him and a sexy smile playing on her lips. She trailed kisses down his belly, over his hip, and down his thigh, teasing around his cock, letting her fingertips tickle his balls. And then she found the head of his cock with her mouth, took it in oh so slowly. He sighed with pleasure, sagging against the wall.

She worked him over with her tongue, her lips, her

hands. Stroking and licking and coaxing him to the edge, then pulling him back. He was so mesmerized by the sight of her beautiful face next to his cock, he could hardly breathe, but then she'd do some indescribably good thing to it and he'd have to gasp for air.

When his legs were nearly shaking and he feared he would fall down if she pleasured him any longer, she placed a soft kiss on the head of his dick and looked up at him with her eyes all soft and seductive.

"I want you," she said. Her voice, breathless and low, spoke volumes as she slid a condom on him.

As if they were one body split in two, desperate to rejoin, he pulled her to a standing position, then lifted her against the wall and plunged into her without a moment of hesitation. Her flesh enveloping him eased the aching so thoroughly that he nearly cried out in relief, and he could only rest still there for a while, savoring it.

Ethan held her hips, with her legs clasped around his waist, and he began pumping into her, using the wall to brace them. Slowly at first to find their rhythm and balance, and faster the surer he became. She devoured him with hungry kisses and greedy hands. There was no stopping, no thinking, only feeling and wanting and needing.

Only this, only them, only right now.

He felt a fast orgasm coming on, and he both

wanted to stop and wanted to sink into it. *Stop it,* his conscious self commanded, while his primitive self was not listening to reason.

Somehow they ended up on the floor, and Ethan was sprawled out on the beige shag carpeting. The unstoppable orgasm, miraculously halted in its tracks by their tumble to the floor, lurked near the edge of his desire, and Nicole hovered over him, straddling his hips as she kissed his neck and chest.

His cock lingered near the nexus of her thighs, but was painfully not there. So close, but not. Any other time, he would have relaxed and enjoyed her teasing, but now he had the single-mindedness of a man dying of hunger. He grasped her hips and guided her where she needed to be, thrust into her again, and held her there for the ride.

The floor was his leverage now as he pumped faster and faster, delirious with the hot wet sensation of her, intoxicated by her scent and her beauty. Her face over his, pleasure softening it, was captivating. He could not look away. And he could see her climax building there. In the tension of her brow, the clouding of her eyes, and that sight pushed him closer and closer to his own orgasm.

But he wanted to delay the inevitable a while longer, so he wrapped his arms around her and rolled her until he was on top, and she was resting on the ground beneath him, her legs hugging his hips. Now he could take his time and savor the pleasure.

Or so he'd thought. No sooner was he thrusting into her again than he felt the delicious way her body enveloped him in this position, and he couldn't help thrusting faster and faster, like a well-oiled machine performing the one task it knew how to do. He gazed into her eyes again, locked here, unable to look away.

He felt an enormous rush of pleasure rising up from his groin, enveloping him, gripping him in its hold, wracking his body. And then he became aware that she was coming too. Her cries of pleasure, her intensely wet pussy swelling around his cock, her eyes closed for the rush.

And it seemed to go on forever, for both of them. By the time he felt his body calm, he was drenched in sweat and breathless, with Nicole collapsed like a rag doll beneath him, just as sweaty and overwhelmed as he.

This wasn't normal sex. It was supernatural sex. Superhuman sex. Sex of epic proportions.

NICOLE WOKE UP feeling as if someone had beaten her. There were aches in her shoulders, her arms, her back, her legs… She stretched beneath the covers, testing each body part to see just how stiff and sore it was before moving on to the next.

And in flashes, the memories came back to her. The nightclub, the car, the police officer, the foyer, the rest of her apartment. They'd had so much sex last night, she'd gotten a killer workout. Her foot bumped against something warm—him.

Ethan.

Still in her bed. Dear God.

And more memories came to her. The fuzzy-headedness, the uncontrollable desire, the absolute certainty that she would die if she wasn't satisfied immediately. She lay staring at Ethan's bare shoulder, the curves and angles of his back, and she tried to remember more.

It all felt like an extremely lucid dream. So strange, so unlike her real self…

The lust potion—could it have been real?

She laughed to herself, silently, then wriggled deeper beneath her down comforter, waiting for her body to wake up. She had not anticipated waking up next to Ethan, a man she probably had nothing in common with outside of certain uncontrollable urges.

And what could they possibly say about last night?

Words fell short. And words confused the truth, which was…what?

Nicole thought of the tiny vial of potion, the claims that it was an aphrodisiac. It seemed impossible that the mere scent of some mystery liquid could induce such a wild reaction in the two of them. Impossible, but…

No, this had to be stress. Ethan had been sniffing around her for as long as she'd known him, and after their first sad little incident in bed, he'd been dying for another chance to prove himself the virile male. So that explained his side of it. As for herself, she'd been having one of the most unpleasant days of her career. She had to forgive herself if the unwinding from it got a little out of hand.

Okay, a lot out of hand.

She was wide awake now, so she eased out of bed and tiptoed across the room. Why couldn't her first and only one-night stand have been with a guy who had the grace to slip out of her apartment in the middle of the night, never to be heard from again?

She didn't need any pretense, no phone calls afterward, nothing. Not for this kind of one-faceted relationship.

Nicole simply didn't do one-night stands. And she had no idea how to handle it now that she had. She wanted to run away from her indiscretion, or have it run away from her.

She entered the bathroom and closed the door silently, flipped on the light and did her business, grabbed a robe, put it on. Maybe she should be the one to slip out of the apartment unnoticed. She could leave the obligatory thanks-for-the-good-time-and-help-yourself-out-the-door note, then stay gone until he left.

Okay, that worked. She could do that. She brushed her teeth as quietly as she could, pulled her hair back in a ponytail and went out into the bedroom to find some clothes. Instead, she found Ethan sitting up in bed, rubbing his eyes.

Crap.

Time for Plan B. Well, except she didn't have a Plan B.

And that's when she noticed that the crazy magnetism she'd felt last night was…perhaps…gone. It was like waking up after having a cold and realizing that the cold wasn't there anymore.

Sure, she could look at Ethan and see that he was an attractive guy. And she'd always felt a certain sort of…something…in his presence. But it was the same as she felt with any guy who was clearly such a reveler in his ability to charm women.

"Hi," he finally said, breaking the awkward silence that had filled the space between them.

"You're awake," she said stupidly.

"As are you." He smiled that dazzling smile, which had a certain quality when softened by the fuzziness of morning.

"I thought you'd be gone by now."

His left eyebrow quirked upward, but he said nothing.

"I mean—" Nicole walked to the dresser and found some panties and a top. "I just figured we were both, you know, letting off steam. That's all."

"To be frank, I didn't really think about what we were doing last night. I felt like I was…possessed, you know?"

She nodded. Did she ever know.

"But," he paused, looked down at himself, "wow, this morning I'm not feeling that crazy...you know."

"Yeah, me either. I guess we just needed to get it out of our systems, right?"

"Maybe so."

Ethan leaned back against the headboard, settling in instead of moving toward the door as she wanted him to. Nicole bit her lip and took off the robe, put on the panties and stretchy tank top, pulled open a bottom drawer where she found a pair of black yoga capris and put those on, too. Dressed, she ignored Ethan and headed for the kitchen, where her coffeepot beckoned.

She went through the motions of making coffee, and when she got it started and left the kitchen, she spotted her cell phone lying on the dining room table and marveled at the fact that it hadn't rung. She usually couldn't make it through an entire Friday night uninterrupted, but her co-workers must have been tiptoeing around her, giving her a break knowing her state of mind.

The coffee gurgled from the kitchen, and she picked up her mail from yesterday, flipped through it one more time. She could hear Ethan moving around in the bedroom now, or maybe the bathroom. Then the shower started, and she breathed a sigh of relief that at least while he was there, she didn't have to talk to him.

Bills, bills, junk mail and bills. She tossed the mail back on the table, and out of the corner of her eye, she caught sight of something red on the patio. She walked across the room, and slid open the vertical blinds. Then she saw that the red was the skirt on a doll, and out of nowhere her stomach recoiled at the sight.

She opened the sliding door, and saw clearly that it was a voodoo doll like the cheesy little things they sold at the tourist shops. It wore a white top, across which were scrawled the words *Die Bitch.*

Nicole's breath whooshed out of her and she slammed the sliding door shut and locked it. She scanned the balcony to see if anything else looked out of place, but no, nothing. Then she peered out at the grounds she could see from her vantage point, and she saw no one, nothing amiss.

"Damn it," she muttered. Her heart was thudding violently in her chest now, and any sense of relaxation she might have gotten from last night had vanished in an instant.

Was this a joke? No, definitely not. An accident, wrong balcony? Doubtful. A sign that Jonas Pulatski had already set his sights on her?

That last thought left her cold, and it resonated with truth. She'd known it was possible he'd seek her out, but she'd never thought it would happen so fast.

She went to the end table and picked up the phone, dialed her office. A few rings later, the department receptionist was on the line, and Nicole explained what had happened and asked for someone to come out and file a report right away.

When she hung up the phone, her heart was still thudding wildly, too fast, and she had a weird fuzzy sensation in her head again. Ethan had turned off the shower, and she went back to the kitchen and poured herself a cup of coffee, then one for him too. Her hands shook.

"I realized belatedly I should have asked first before using your shower," Ethan said from behind her, and she turned to find him standing in the kitchen doorway.

She burst into tears, which was even more out of character for her than what she'd done last night.

7

ETHAN TOOK NICOLE into his arms and held her against his chest, baffled by her burst of tears but instinctively wanting to comfort her. Had the shower usage really been such a huge offense?

Or was it something else? Was she suffering from huge regrets about last night?

Her close proximity brought back a rush of desire so strong, his cock went instantly hard, and he had to shift his weight away from her down there just to avoid poking her at this inopportune time.

He smoothed her hair and rubbed her back as he held her, and once she'd calmed a bit, he asked, "What is it? What's bothering you?"

She pushed away and took a deep breath, wiped the dampness from her eyes. Then she pointed at the balcony, and he walked over to it, his gut twisting at the thought that maybe he'd accidentally left some evidence that he'd been hiding there yesterday.

Ethan reached the glass door and stared at the weird

little voodoo doll, and a rush of guilt and recognition and confusion hit him in the chest.

What the hell?

It looked a lot like the voodoo doll Zoe had bought at the tourist shop yesterday. How had it gotten there? And why on God's earth did it have to appear on the balcony right after he'd done his little pervert impression in that very spot?

"What's the matter?" Nicole asked. "You look like—"

"Like I just saw a creepy little voodoo doll with a death threat scrawled across its chest in blood?" His faux light tone came out sounding as fake as it really was, and he forced out a laugh in a failed attempt to cover it up.

She frowned at him. "Yeah…" she said, sounding unconvinced. "I'm freaked out too. There's an officer headed over now to take a report."

"Do you think it's—"

"Yes, definitely. But it's odd. My neighbor claimed to have seen someone on my balcony yesterday— someone driving a car that fits your description."

"Wow, that's more than odd. That's downright freaky," he choked out.

Ethan paced across the room and back again, pausing at the balcony door. What could he do now? Admit the truth, that he'd been lurking around on her balcony yesterday, right before someone had just happened to leave the doll there? Could the angry neighbor have left the doll as some kind of warped retaliation?

He imagined Nicole's reaction to his story and decided that no, no way in hell could he admit the truth. He'd just have to take his chances.

Nicole went into another room and came back with a camera and a plastic bag that turned out to contain an evidence kit. She put on gloves and went out onto the patio, then carefully knelt down next to the doll and took a few shots of it, before collecting it up in a bag.

Ethan watched all this in a state of abject misery, not quite sure whether to bolt from the apartment completely, confess the truth, or stick around for the horror show to begin.

But then his self-preservation instincts got out of the way so he could see the real problem at hand—that some sicko had put such a thing on Nicole's patio in the first place. She was clearly a woman who knew how to take care of herself, but still, he couldn't stand the thought that she was in danger, that someone out there truly wished her harm.

"Do you have any neighbors who might have, you know, just done this as a dirty trick for some weird reason? A parking spot conflict or something?"

She looked up at him. "Not that I can think of. I get along with all my neighbors. This is a pretty friendly building."

Ethan bit his tongue to keep from pointing out that at least one of her neighbors wielded a baseball bat with a little too much abandon for his taste.

There was a knock at the door, and Nicole went to open it. The doorway was filled by a large officer in uniform, and he and Nicole talked for a short bit before he entered and went about the work of taking a report.

Ethan went into the kitchen and helped himself to some coffee, growing more and more uncomfortable as the minutes ticked by, having to omit the little detail of lurking around on Nicole's balcony. But then he thought again of the downstairs neighbor. She was totally going to squeal on him when questioned.

And then what?

Nicole would recognize his description and determine that he was the sick jerk responsible for the voodoo doll. Maybe they'd even trace it back to the tourist trap where Zoe had bought that doll, and then the whole thing would definitely point to him, and he'd go to prison for years and have forced unnatural relationships with that guy named Bubba.

It was all too horrifying to contemplate.

He had to tell them the truth. But no freaking way could he do it.

He went back into the living room with his coffee, to find that the police officer was wrapping up his report and Nicole was promising to give him a call if she thought of anything else. So would he go talk to the neighbors right now?

Ethan kept his mouth shut until after the officer had left, and then he cleared his throat.

"I've, um, got a little confession to make," he said.

Nicole's brow furrowed as she looked at him. "Okay, what is it?"

"This is going to sound completely bizarre, and I didn't have the balls to bring it up while the police officer was here, but the truth is, I was on your balcony for a short while yesterday."

Her eyes widened, and he wondered if she was going to slap him.

"I swear I had nothing to do with that doll, and it wasn't there when I was on the balcony. I promise you that."

She took a step back, and then another. Ethan glanced behind her at the purse that lay on her dining room table. She probably kept a gun in it, and she was probably going to shoot him in the kneecaps for doing what he'd done, if he didn't do a really fabulous job of explaining why the hell he'd done it.

And why the bloody hell *had* he done it?

"What were you doing on my balcony?"

"It's hard to explain."

She crossed her arms over her chest and took another backward step in the direction of the purse.

Ethan felt a premature pain in his knees. "Do you

remember how crazed we felt yesterday? Like we couldn't get enough of each other?"

Her eyes narrowed, but she nodded.

"Well, I, um, got so possessed with that feeling, I thought I might go crazy if I let you out of my sight."

"And?"

"I followed you home, thinking I wanted to talk to you about the tension between us, but somewhere along the way I just got so caught up in watching you, it was like I was possessed or something. I got so frustrated that I climbed onto your balcony and watched you through the window."

"You stupid mother—"

"Just hear me all the way out, please," he said, holding up his hands. "I was absolutely not thinking clearly. I really believe that lust potion affected my brain somehow. Maybe it really is a narcotic of some sort, like you said."

"Then why was I able to go my merry way home without feeling the need to stalk *you?*"

One more step closer to the bag. She'd probably be aiming a gun at him any second now.

"Maybe the stuff has a slightly different effect depending on the person."

"Or maybe I'm not a lunatic who lurks around on people's balconies!" She reached for the phone on a nearby table, grabbed it, and started dialing. "I have to add this information to the police report, you know."

"Just please wait. Hear me out first, then decide what to do, okay?"

She eyed him warily, hit the phone's off button, and sighed. "You've got two minutes to convince me you're not a lunatic. Then I'm calling."

"I really had no control over following you. In my head I knew it was crazy, but I couldn't stop myself. Just like what happened between us last night. I know if you could have stopped yourself, you probably would have, right?"

A little scowl crossed her face. It was partly that attitude of hers that he loved so much. He knew she didn't take crap from anyone, and especially not from guys fixated on getting into her pants.

"We've already discussed this," she finally said.

"But you did feel that crazy thing I'm talking about."

Another sigh. "Yes. I felt it."

"And it's not nearly as strong today, is it?"

"I guess since we're not still attacking each other, that's a yes."

"I did feel it again when I was hugging you, but I don't know, it also could have just been my usual reaction to a beautiful woman in my arms."

She smirked. "You got hard while I was crying on your shoulder. Typical, Ethan."

"I'm sorry. So you didn't feel any arousal at that moment?" Stupid guy question, he realized only after the words had exited his mouth.

An awkward pause, and then she said slowly, "Well, um…actually, I kind of did. Which surprised me, given the circumstances."

"I think it's just some kind of uncontrollable reaction we're having. It was the same with climbing onto your balcony. I would have stopped myself if I could."

"I don't know. It sounds pretty damn weird if you ask me."

"Yeah. At least today, I cannot even imagine following you home and climbing up there to watch you."

"Why are you telling me all this now? Why not just keep quiet since you didn't get caught?" She was still looking at him as though he was something stuck to the bottom of her shoe, which wasn't exactly what he'd call progress.

"I kind of did get caught. Your downstairs neighbor spotted me and chased me with a baseball bat."

"Anita? So she really did spot you and your car." The look of disgust was gone now, replaced by mild amusement.

"That would be her. She got a few pretty good swipes at my car while she was at it."

"She's a one-woman neighborhood watch and lynch mob all rolled into one. She also sees things that aren't there when she forgets to take her medication, so I wasn't sure I could believe her."

"I'm sorry I lied to you."

Nicole full-on smiled. "So you're afraid if the police question her, she'll tattle on you. That's what prompted you to be honest?"

"Can you think of any other reason I should admit to having done a peeping-tom routine?"

"Because you're a freak?"

Well, there was that.

"Yes, I'm a freak and I want to make sure you know it so that I can be arrested pronto. Makes perfect sense to me."

"I think you need to go now," Nicole said, and Ethan felt a stab of regret in his belly.

Definitely not the reaction he was hoping for, but at least she wasn't reaching for the phone again. Progress!

Yeah. Um. Right.

"There's one other strange thing about yesterday—if you can believe it."

Nicole eyed him but said nothing.

"I went to a little tourist trap shop yesterday during my lunch hour with a couple of friends, and the place sold voodoo dolls. One of my friends even bought a doll, though it looked different than the one that was on your balcony."

She sighed wearily. "This just keeps getting better and better," she said, then paused, appearing to mull over the new facts. "Did you get any sense of hostility from Pulatski when you interviewed him?"

"Not especially, but he wasn't friendly, either. Why?"

"Maybe he followed you, for whatever reason. Maybe he sees you as a threat, or an easy target."

Ethan had put himself in a few dangerous situations over the years while following a story, so he wouldn't have been surprised to have an ex-convict on his tail. But it wasn't exactly a comforting thought, either.

"But—"

"Not another word. Just go. I need to think about this some more, and add these new details to the report."

Ethan glanced at the couch, where some of his clothes were draped over the back from last night. He started gathering his things, finishing getting dressed, putting his shoes on. All the while wondering if there was anything he could say to change her mind.

Maybe not. At least not right now. She probably needed some space to assimilate things, but...

"Are you really going to feel okay being here alone after that voodoo doll?"

"I have friends I can call to come over, or I can go stay with someone," she said tightly.

"Okay, um, I guess I'll be going then. But I'd feel better leaving after you have someone else here with you."

"I've got Anita and her baseball bat downstairs, and a 35 mm handgun in my purse. I'll be fine. Now get the hell out."

8

OKAY, SO SHE'D LIED. She'd had no intention of running and hiding behind her friends just because some asshole had left a voodoo doll on her balcony. Nicole couldn't stand running for cover over every little scare. It was a sign of weakness, and she was determined not to be a weak woman. She was the kind of person people ran to when they needed help, not the other way around.

But a night of clutching her gun under her pillow and jumping at every little noise and sleeping a total of two hours had taught her a lesson about her own bravery. It seemed to have disappeared.

And she was ashamed of that.

A colleague had called her late Saturday evening to tell her that while there hadn't been any fingerprints on the doll, a second note had been found inside of it. It had been a paper list of police officers who'd died on duty in the past few years, including her own former partner who'd been killed by Pulatski. And then there was her name, at the bottom of the list, with Ethan's name beside it.

That was the most perplexing part of all. If the perpetrator was Pulatski, what was he doing putting Ethan's name on the list, and what did it mean? Had Ethan pissed him off somehow during the interview he'd done while Pulatski was still in prison? Had he not really wanted the kind of news coverage Ethan was going to give him, and determined that a dead journalist would be better than a talking one?

If Ethan had been following Nicole Friday, had gone so far as climbing onto her balcony, and Jonas had been watching, he might have seen the perfect opportunity to make things tough on Ethan, at least for a little while, by planting the voodoo doll right where Ethan had been seen lurking.

She'd had to divulge her relationship with Ethan to the detective who'd called, and they'd discussed the possibility that Jonas had spotted Ethan at her apartment.

And so now she had to protect Ethan from his own stupidity. It was Sunday morning, and she was tired and grumpy from lack of sleep, on edge from the whole voodoo doll incident, and fill with a vague sense of dread.

She got herself showered and dressed, feeling guilty now, too, that she hadn't thought to call Ethan last night to warn him that he might be in danger. Yet another example of how she hadn't been herself for the past couple of days. She was about to pick up the phone to call Ethan when she heard a knock at her door.

Through the peephole, she saw Cal Mendelson, the same detective with whom she'd spoken last night. Salt-and-pepper hair, permanent worry lines and a chain-smoking habit were evidence of the twenty years he'd put in on the force. She unlocked the dead bolts on her door and opened it, feeling comforted to see one of her most trusted colleagues there, live and in the flesh, after such a long night.

"Hey, Cal, what's up?" she said, motioning him in.

"Mind if I sit?" he asked, shrugging off his black windbreaker and tossing it over the back of the couch.

"Sure." Nicole sat down on the opposite end of the couch before belatedly thinking to offer him a drink. "Want some coffee? A soft drink?"

"No thanks. I was just driving by to check up on things. I needed to talk to you about the Pulatski case."

"Any more leads turn up?"

Cal shook his head. "The address he gave his parole officer appears to be unoccupied now, and no one seems to know where he's gone."

"So at least we can get him on a parole violation, if nothing else."

"Right. Once we track him down, that is. But in the meantime, I'm worried about your safety, and I have an idea I want to run past you."

"Okay, shoot," Nicole said, leaning back against the couch and pulling her legs up under her.

"Everyone down at the precinct would understand if you took a little time off, given your situation."

"Is that why I haven't gotten any calls on my cell phone all weekend?"

"I asked people not to bother you. I really think you'd do well to lay low until we catch up with Pulatski again."

"I'm not sure I can handle just sitting around doing nothing, when I know I could be out there helping find him."

"That's the thing though," Cal said. "You can help by keeping an eye on your reporter friend—the one on that list."

"Ethan?" How did Cal know Ethan was a so-called friend? Had the officer who'd caught them Friday night already blabbed to the entire goddamn San Diego PD?

Shit.

"You want me to be his bodyguard or something?"

"If you want to call it that. Just stick around him, keep an eye out. Strength in numbers and all that."

"I don't know," Nicole said, hating the idea already. "Couldn't we just have a patrol car follow him around?"

"We want something a little less obvious than that. Pulatski's no fool. He made sure there were no fingerprints on that doll, but he clearly wrote the note inside in his own handwriting. I think he was trying to send us a message—in more ways than one."

"You got the handwriting analysis back already?"

Cal nodded. "Just this morning. I put a rush on it."

"So it's the usual story. Instead of rehabilitating the scumbag, prison turned Jonas into an even bigger one, huh?"

"Seems that way. He was a small-time thug before he went in, but talking to some of the inmates, he stayed pretty angry the whole time he served his sentence."

She shook her head. "So of course we let him back out on the street."

"The problem with Jonas is that he's smart—way smarter than the average scumbag. He was known on the inside for masterminding drug deals, a couple of riots, and even an attack on a prison guard that left the guy in critical condition. But he managed to avoid leaving any real evidence that he was behind the shit."

"Great," she said. She'd heard bits and pieces of his prison activities, but she'd mostly blocked it out. "So he's all set up for a big-time life of crime unless we cut him off at the pass."

Nicole bit her lip, contemplating how bad it might look if she really did take time off right now. It would make her look weak, incapable of handling the stressors that went hand in hand with her profession.

"I don't think my taking time off right now is a good idea."

"Nicole, everyone knows how tough you are. You don't have anything left to prove, okay? You proved yourself years ago when you braved the aftermath of Max's death without ever flinching."

She blinked away the stinging sensation in her eyes. Not crumbling after Max died had taken drawing from her deepest reservoirs of strength, and even then she'd felt as if she was nearly comatose, going through the motions without really being alive for a while.

As a woman, it was a constant struggle to prove herself in such a male-dominated world. And not just a woman, but a woman like Nicole knew she was at heart—the soft, emotional, impassioned sort. The kind that usually didn't survive in police work. Somehow, she had managed for this long, and she wouldn't lose it now.

She wouldn't let her family history be her undoing. She might have come from a long line of women who'd failed, who'd been undone by the men in their lives, but she would rise above that. She knew that some perverse part of her had even sought out success in a male-dominated arena just to confirm to herself that she could not only avoid being undone by men, but that she could thrive among them.

"Are people talking about…" Friday night. She couldn't say it though.

"About the Pulatski case? Sure, a little."

Maybe the officer who'd caught them Friday night hadn't blabbed after all. Miraculous, if it was true.

"No other weird rumors about me or anything?"

"You're a hell of a lot more respected than you

realize, Nicole. No one's going to think twice about you being out of the office for a little while, and if anyone asks, I'll just say you're on a special assignment, which is pretty much true, right?"

"So is it a leave of absence or a special assignment, for real?"

"We'll call it whatever makes you feel okay about going along with the idea."

Nicole sighed. She could have argued more, but the truth was she wanted to make sure Ethan was safe, and she could do that best if she was close by. And while it pained her to admit it to herself, she really didn't want to be alone right now.

"Okay," she said grudgingly. "You've talked me into it. Now I've got to get Ethan to go along with the idea though."

Cal smiled. "Somehow I doubt he'll have a problem accepting you as his bodyguard."

Nicole's stomach went queasy. "Is there something you're not telling me?"

"No, I just meant, I mean…" Cal stuttered. "I assumed you two are a couple, if Jonas somehow spotted you hanging around together."

"Oh. Not exactly. I mean, it's more like we're, you know, acquaintances."

"Good. You deserve better than some pain-in-the-ass reporter, anyway."

Ethan's reputation was apparently well-known

around the precinct. Pain in the ass was an understatement, but Nicole did have to respect his commitment to his work, his drive to keep the public informed. And he was one of the few reporters she'd ever dealt with who hadn't taken her words and twisted them to fit the angle the reporter wanted to take on the story.

"I've got to go run an errand now," Nicole said, wanting to get to the pharmacy before it closed. She'd let her birth control prescription lapse since her last relationship ended, but having sex with Ethan Friday night had been a wake-up call to get off her ass and go pick up some pills. The pharmacy closed at noon on Sundays, so she needed to get moving. "But I'll stop and talk to Ethan on the way. I'll do my best to convince him," she said, before realizing too late how bad that might sound.

To his credit, Cal kept a straight face. "Everyone around the precinct is concerned about you, Nicole. We just want to make sure you're okay, so don't hesitate to ask for anything if you need it. You've got my cell number—use it, okay?"

She nodded. "I will, I promise."

"I've got plainclothes cops keeping an eye on your place and Ethan's. We'll catch Pulatski—don't worry. Sooner or later he's going to trip up."

Nicole nodded and stood up as Cal put on his jacket and headed for the door. Once he was gone, she grabbed her purse and put on her shoes, then hurried out the door herself. If Ethan agreed to let her hang around him 24/7, she'd have to come back later to pack some things to stay at his place. There was no way she'd allow him to stay here for a prolonged period of time—she'd have no place to escape to if Ethan started driving her crazy.

She had a contact card he'd given her in her purse, and when she dug it out, she recognized the street. Twenty minutes later she was pulling into his driveway, her insides jittery for reasons she didn't want to examine at the moment.

Nicole peered out the car window at 3915 Rio Los Altos, and she sighed. This was Ethan's house, then. This was the place where she would have to spend God-knew-how-long holed up playing bodyguard. That is, if she could get him to cooperate.

His house was not exactly what she'd imagined. She supposed she'd have labeled him a postmodern condo dweller. Instead, he occupied a small, low-slung Spanish bungalow with a white stucco exterior, a red-tile roof, and a series of three arches leading onto the front porch. A corner house, it sat at the intersection of two minor residential streets lined with palms and oleander bushes.

Security-wise, the place was a wreck. Lots of unsecured street-level windows and easy hiding spots for lurkers. She made a mental note to recommend he get some decorative grating to cover the windows and keep out the less-determined crooks. She exited her car and walked up the sidewalk, taking everything in, noting each and every detail, from the flimsy-looking screen door on the front to the single lock on the maple door.

Instead of ringing the doorbell, she kept walking around to the side of the house, noting more details, observing every entry point a criminal might use. By the time she'd made it to the unlatched gate to the backyard, she could hear a shower running through an open window. In the back, she checked the sliding glass door and found it unlocked.

Frowning, she slid the door open, and peeked inside. From the living room, she could hear a stereo playing an old Depeche Mode song, and the shower still ran in a bathroom somewhere down the hallway. She stepped into the dining room area, which Ethan had made into a sort of office complete with an old rolltop desk. The only thing that hinted dining room was the pair of bar stools that sat under the bar dividing the kitchen from the room where she stood.

Okay, so she probably shouldn't have been trespassing, but she had a point to make about Ethan's safety, or lack thereof, and his clearly idiotic sense of comfort with unsecured doors. He didn't exactly live in the safest neighborhood, and he was showering with his sliding glass door unlocked. It was like inviting drug addicts in to beat him and take his stuff.

Or worse. Because Jonas Pulatski was far less

predictable than a drug addict, and probably more dangerous.

Nicole could hear singing now too, as she walked closer to the sound of the shower. Ethan was singing, bizarrely, an off-key rendition of Patsy Cline's "Crazy."

She bit her lip to keep from laughing. A glance around the living room revealed more of his everyday life. A few photos of smiling people that must have been friends or family members on the mantel, a worn-out Persian rug on the floor and a couple of mod brown leather sofas that had probably been around since the early eighties, were the first clues she noticed.

A small TV—the boxy outdated kind—sat forlornly in one corner of the room, ignored by the sofas, which were grouped around the fireplace. Not that anyone really needed a fireplace in San Diego, but they were nice to have nonetheless, and Nicole was fascinated that Ethan was probably a guy who didn't watch much TV.

Having seen the various men in her mother's life camp out in front of the TV for days on end as a kid, she'd never found it an attractive trait in a guy. In fact, it drove her insane.

She took note of the magazines and books strewn across the coffee table, ranging from ragged copies of *The Economist* to a hardcover mystery to a huge book of contemporary art.

So Ethan was not only a horn dog, but also a bit of an intellectual. Or at least a Euro intellectual. Maybe that was just more par-for-the-course in England. He was, after all, a journalist, which involved using his brain.

Nicole had never thought to wonder why he'd ended up all the way across the world, in San Diego. She'd just accepted him as a foreign-accented pain in her ass, as expected as the changing of the tides and bird droppings on park benches.

But now, standing in his living room, she did wonder. One of the photos on his mantel showed a glimpse of Big Ben behind the four smiling women in the photo. One of them was an older woman, maybe even Ethan's mother, and the other three looked to be in their twenties or thirties. They all bore some resemblance to Ethan— brown hair, blue eyes, a way of smiling a little crooked. Sisters, maybe. He had three of them?

Nicole had three sisters of her own. They were all in various states of divorce or separation from various loser guys. All three had kids they couldn't handle, problems they couldn't deal with, bills they couldn't pay. It was the story of the Arroyo women for as far back as she could remember.

Not exactly a proud history, but Nicole was determined, above all else, to be the first one to overcome it.

So far, so good. With Friday night being a notable exception.

She shook herself out of the daze she'd sunken into staring at the photo of the women, and a second later she heard the water shut off. Ethan had wrapped up his Patsy Cline impersonation. Too bad. She would have loved to catch him in the midst of it, but she hadn't wanted to give him a heart attack by sneaking up while he was in the shower. Thanks to Hitchcock, people tended to freak out more than was warranted when surprised in showers.

Nicole moved silently down the hallway, her hands in the combat-ready position just in case she upset Ethan so much he tried to throttle her. She almost wanted to laugh, but she was pissed off enough at his lack of street smarts leaving the door unlocked that she was able to get rid of the urge.

She paused at the bathroom doorway, and took a deep breath. The door stood slightly ajar, and she could hear only a shuffling sound that she imagined was Ethan drying himself off. She had a flash of guilt that she was invading his privacy this way, but better her than some sick scumbag criminal with a gun in hand doing it.

Then she heard water running again, this time in the sink, she guessed. Next came the buzz of a razor. In a flash of motion, Nicole pushed open the door and burst into the room.

"Hands on top of your head," she shouted.

Ethan's razor went sailing across the room and thunked against the wall as he spun around, his arms hovering somewhere between over his head and ready to defend himself.

"What the—?"

"You left your goddamn door unlocked. What the hell were you thinking?" she shouted.

His expression, confused and bewildered, transformed into recognition and then exasperation. "What are you doing checking my house for unlocked doors? Couldn't get enough of me and had to come back for more? You could have knocked—I'd have let you in."

And in that instant, he was back to his usual smirking self. Only his usual self was wearing nothing but a towel, and his hair was tousled and damp, and beads of water glistened on his shoulders, begging her to lick them off…

Out of nowhere a new wave of arousal swept through Nicole, and it occurred to her that she was completely screwed. Here she was trying to teach Ethan a safety lesson, and all she could think of was ripping off his towel and licking him dry.

Silence hung in the air between them for a moment too long, and she could tell by the certainty in his expression that he knew he had her number, even when she hadn't realized what she was doing.

Damn it.

"You're so full of shit," she said, not sounding quite as convincing as she would have liked. "I came over here because of police business, and I couldn't stand by and let you leave your doors unlocked when your life is at risk."

That now-familiar wave of tingling took a sweep through her lower abdomen, welling up in her panties and then swirling around there until she inhaled at the growing intensity of it.

That stupid potion—she made a mental note to put a rush on the analysis of it.

Or was she just *that* sex-starved?

He was frowning at her now. "What police business?"

"I need to talk to you about Pulatski."

He nodded. "Sure. What's up?"

"We have reason to believe he's targeted us both, and I think I should kind of act as your bodyguard while we're looking for him."

"A what?"

"A bodyguard. You're in danger, Ethan. You need protection."

"The only protection I need is made of lubricated rubber and comes in a little square packet. Really, Nicole—"

"Don't get all macho on me now. This isn't the time for it. Jonas Pulatski is a loose cannon."

"And what did you mean about while *we're* looking for him? We're not going on a manhunt, are we? Because I have deadlines at work."

Just like a journalist to think of deadlines before all else, even when he'd just been told his life was in danger.

"I meant *we,* as in the general collective police department. Not you."

"It sounds like you're really the one who needs protecting."

"I've got department surveillance people watching out for me. But I also know how to take care of myself. You, on the other hand, are a person who leaves his patio door unlocked while taking a shower, leaves his car doors unlocked, leaves his windows unlocked—"

"Okay, okay. I didn't realize I'd have a crazed lunatic stalking me. I got a little lax, I'll admit."

"It's not just the unlocked stuff, Ethan. You need someone around who knows what signs to look for that you're in danger."

"And that someone would be you?"

"Yes," she said. She probably should have suggested he hire a professional bodyguard, but she felt responsible for dragging him into this mess with Pulatski.

And yeah, okay, she didn't want to be alone. She hated to admit to herself that she was a little unnerved, but she was. She'd let the stress get to her too much.

Ethan smiled a slow, half-cocked smile. "Oh really? You'd be staying here at my house, twenty-four hours a day?"

Nicole hesitated. Could she really do this?

"Yes, pretty much," she finally said. "It would give me a place to stay besides my own apartment, and then the surveillance people would essentially be watching out for both of us. The only time you'd probably be in danger is when you're at work or going to and from."

"I could probably work from home, if I knew you were here. Or maybe I'd be doing everything but working if you were here…."

Nicole sighed. "This isn't about us having sex, Ethan. It's about staying alive."

"For the sexiest cop I've ever met, you sure know how to be a wet blanket."

"For a crime reporter, you sure know how to be a dumb-ass," she shot back.

Ethan smiled again, as usual not even the least bit fazed by her hostility. That pissed her off even more than the way he turned her on—the fact that she couldn't ruffle him as he was ruffling her.

"You can be my bodyguard so long as you promise to guard me very, very closely."

She blinked, surprised he was giving in so easily. "Okay…"

"But there will be ground rules," he said oh so casually.

"Of course, like—"

"*My* ground rules. You sleep in my bed, you stick with me 24/7, and you continue our, ah, physical relationship."

Nicole laughed, not because she thought he was funny, but because he'd caught her utterly and completely off guard. "You expect me to sleep with you so I can protect you?"

He nodded. "That pretty much covers it, yep."

"Go screw yourself." She turned on her heels and headed toward the front door. "You can hire a rent-a-cop for all I care," she called over her shoulder.

But Ethan followed her, and dodged around her before she could get to the door. He put himself between her and it, and if she'd been a little bit madder she'd have kicked him in the balls to move him out of the way. But he was wearing that expression of his, somewhere between self-deprecating and apologetic, that had an uncanny ability to make her forget what she was pissed off about.

"You're really going to trust my safety to a rent-a-cop?"

"Yep," she said, but she wasn't feeling much conviction at the moment.

"I offered up those conditions for you, too, you know. The more we're together, the more we can watch each other's back."

"Not if we're busy screwing all the time, we can't."

"So you admit it. You do want to shag me all the time, don't you?"

"Hell no." Again, not sounding very convincing. Damn it.

But she could still feel that magnetic pull toward Ethan. She could remember the mind-blowing sex, the orgasms like she'd never had before, the sheer euphoria of their night together, and she had to admit, she wanted more of it.

A whole lot more of it.

Who wouldn't? She was a healthy female with healthy female needs that didn't get met nearly often enough. And so what if she decided to let her needs get met by a guy she heretofore could hardly stand to be around? He had his charms. Very obvious charms, really. Not the least of which was his stunning ability to please her in bed, and in the backseat of the car, and probably anywhere else, too.

"Tell me that wasn't the best sex of your life Friday night."

"It wasn't the best sex of my life," she lied. "It was nice, but…"

His smile grew. "When you lie, you look over my shoulder. It's so obvious. I figured a police detective would know how to tell tales better, after seeing so many criminals do it."

But Nicole was basically an honest person. She had never had any desire to learn how to deceive, and while she could recognize a lie from a scumbag she'd dragged in off the street in half a second, it didn't translate to her own ability to be a liar or a cheat.

"Okay," she said, looking him dead in the eye. "The sex was great. You know it and I know it. Is that what you wanted me to say?"

"No, I'm still waiting for the 'it was the best sex of my life' statement."

"You're going to rot before you hear that one."

"So you can't admit it, but it's true. You were trembling as we made love. Your whole body trembling, and you were so wet you could have given us both a bath in—"

"Classy, Ethan. Keep up that kind of sweet talk. It's what every girl loves to hear," she said sarcastically.

"I'm just telling you what I observed. You were enjoying it in a huge way, Nicole."

She couldn't argue with him there. It really had been the best sex of her life—sex better than she could have imagined possible—but no way was she going to admit *that*.

Not to Ethan. Not in a million years.

"As were you. Best sex of *your* life, yes? I'm sure we can both agree on that."

He laughed. "You're relentless, Nicole Arroyo. That's one of the things I love about you. You just won't give in about being a hard-ass."

"I'm not a hard-ass." But she was, and she knew it. She hated that about herself, hated that being determined and strong in her career had made her hard in every part of her life. But she didn't know how to be any other way and stay focused.

That was the problem with being an Arroyo woman: the temptation to screw up was strong, and she had to fight it at all costs, even at the cost of being a likeable person sometimes.

"Okay, so can't you just agree to really good sex as

part of the deal then? You don't have to admit it was the best of your life, but you can enjoy it for what it is, if we're going to be around each other all the time anyway."

Nicole grasped her last shred of common sense and held on for dear life. "Forget it, Ethan. Sex is not part of the deal."

And with that, she sidestepped him and walked out the door.

9

OKAY, SO SHE'D called his bluff. What the hell. It had been worth a try.

Except…

If he had to choose between having Nicole around him 24/7 or not having her around, he'd take the first option, sex or no sex.

Ethan had entertained himself with countless fantasies since the first time he'd ever gotten a full-on erection, a virtual porn library of fantasies. But he'd never imagined this one—shacked up with a sexy but cantankerous cop, who was supposed to be his bodyguard.

And oh, did his body ever need guarding. He just had to convince Nicole that her job involved less of the boring security stuff—peering out windows and checking for signs of intruders—and more of the type he had in mind. For instance, his cock was feeling rather lonely, perhaps even in danger of neglect, if she didn't occupy his bed tonight.

He stood in the living room blinking at his own

stupidity for a full minute before he realized the opportunity he'd just missed out on. He had a bad habit of letting his Type A control-freak personality rear its ugly head at the most inopportune moments. And he feared he'd just done it again. Why the hell would Nicole have wanted to sleep with him when he was essentially demanding it?

Of course she wouldn't. That's why he made a point of always—well, mostly—trying to come across as easygoing and laid-back. It made women take their panties off.

He could have convinced Nicole to shag him over a few days' time at most. Having her around in such close proximity surely would have resulted in sex, if he'd simply let the situation take its natural course.

But no, he'd gone and turned into a typical guy about the whole thing, practically wanting a written contract that he'd get to screw her to his heart's desire. Could he get any more stupid?

And when a guy had just been told a murderer was likely stalking him, wouldn't it make sense to inquire further about the matter instead of jumping straight to the sex? But he'd seen how mesmerized Nicole had been by him, and he'd felt his own arousal, and he'd skipped right over the murderer part. Now that he was alone, he felt like a fool for his errors.

Outside, the sound of her car engine sprang him into action. He grasped the towel around his waist to keep it secure and took off outside at a full run. Nicole was backing out of the driveway, looking over her shoulder at the road behind her, so she didn't see him until he'd reached the street and she was about to drive forward again.

When she did spot him coming toward her wearing only his towel, she slammed on her brakes and glared at him. A second later, her driver's side window slid down.

"What the hell are you doing?"

"I'm sorry. You're right. If we're both in danger, I'd much rather have you here than anywhere else. Forget the stupid conditions I said before. I was being a jackass."

She narrowed her eyes at him. "If you're thinking the sight of you in a towel is going to change my mind, you're forgetting you've been wearing that thing since I got here."

"I wouldn't presume any such thing. I was just thinking with the wrong head before. Really. I'd feel tons better if you'd stay here with me—for both of us. And I promise, no hanky-panky."

Well, for now. At least for the next four hours or so.

He'd behave. He really would. He'd let her realize on her own that there was no way the two of them could be in the same house without serious sparks flying.

"Please?" he said when she continued to glare silently.

"One screw-up and you'll be looking up rent-a-cops in the phone book, you understand?"

"Absolutely. I'll be the model of good behavior."

Good in bed behavior, that is.

"I have to go run an errand, then go back to my place to get some stuff. You have a guest room?"

"Sure, my extra bedroom has a fold-out couch. You can sleep there."

So long as she let him sleep there with her.

A neighbor, Mrs. Gillespie, drove by in a beige minivan. She had her three kids in the car too, and they all stared at Ethan standing there with his wet hair, bare chest and white towel.

Perfect.

Now he'd be labeled the neighborhood weirdo, and no one would come to his house on Halloween for candy. No, they'd wait until after the trick-or-treaters were gone and then they'd toilet paper his house.

He nodded and waved, as if the whole scene was perfectly normal. Towels were acceptable as far as the end of the driveway, right?

But his waving hand happened to be the same hand he'd been using to hold his towel, and no sooner did he shake his hand at the Gillespies than a gust of wind caught the towel and tugged it loose. Suddenly the Gillespie girls were getting what may have been their first male anatomy lesson.

Nicole burst out laughing. Ethan grabbed for his towel and caught it before it hit the ground, tugged it around his waist, and stood up as tall as he could while he secured it, trying his best to save the last shred of his dignity by appearing unperturbed, which he mostly was. He didn't have anything to be ashamed of under the towel, after all. His dangly bits were more than adequate to suit most women's needs. Or so he'd been told.

"Get back inside before I have to arrest you for public indecency," Nicole said, then rolled up her window and drove away.

SOMETIMES, THERE REALLY WAS poetic justice in life. As a police officer, Nicole had seen far too many instances where justice was never served in the traditional sense. But seeing Ethan standing next to the street with his Johnson dangling in the wind for the world to see was proof that, occasionally, people got what was coming to them one way or another.

Nicole's cell phone rang as she was pulling away from the pharmacy near her apartment. She grabbed it from the passenger seat, checked the number, and saw that it was her sister Gina. She clicked the speakerphone button and put the phone down.

"Hey, I'm driving. Make it quick."

"I'm at your apartment and you're not here. Where the hell are you?" Gina had never been one to mince words.

"I'm like one minute away. Got stuck in a traffic jam, so just chill."

"I don't want to be here alone when you've probably got some stalker lurking around waiting to kill you."

"Then lock your car door. 'Bye, sis." Nicole hit the

phone's hang-up button, and cruised down her block. That's what she got for calling her mom this morning to let her know what was going on—she already had family members descending on her like vultures to get all the latest gossip.

A few seconds later, she was in her parking lot, next to Gina's car, a beat-up old Impala that was a castoff from her first husband.

It was odd, the farther Nicole got from Ethan, the clearer her thoughts felt, and the more she had to wonder how he was any temptation to her at all. She had willpower, so she should be able to apply it to any situation, right?

She got out of the car at the same time as her sister, whose empty rear car seats indicated she must have left the kids with their grandmother or another sitter.

"I finally get free of the rug rats and you make me spend my precious time sitting here waiting for you?" was Gina's greeting.

"I didn't even know you were showing up. You could have called earlier."

"I did. Got no answer. You can't tell Mom there's some guy out to kill you and not expect one of your dear sisters to be sent over to get the scoop."

"Sorry, I forgot gossiping about my life is one of your favorite forms of entertainment." Nicole headed toward the stairwell and climbed it with Gina behind her.

She did feel a lot safer with another warm body

there, even if there was a plainclothes cop parked across the street, and even if Gina was the very sister who'd stood by and let Nicole get beaten up by the class bully in second grade.

Outside her apartment now, she felt exposed, even though logically she knew she was safe in broad daylight with eyewitnesses and a cop watching. But still. She was vulnerable. For the first time in years, Nicole felt as though someone or something could get to her.

She quickly unlocked the front door and went inside, her sister following.

"So what are you doing about this psycho who wants to kill you? You going to go in the witness protection program or something?"

Nicole really needed to stick with her policy of telling her family nothing more often.

"I'm not a witness to any crime, so I don't qualify for the witness protection program," Nicole said as she rolled her eyes at the wall before turning back to Gina. "I'm going to be staying at a friend's house for a while. You can reach me on my cell phone if you need anything."

"Which friend?" Gina could spot potential gossip a mile away.

"Someone you don't know."

"A male friend?"

"Yeah, sort of."

"He's sort of male or sort of a friend?"

"What do you think?"

"I think you're shacking up with some guy! Finally, my little sister is getting her groove on. It's about damn time, you prude."

"I'm not a virgin, you know."

Gina flopped down on the couch and put her feet up on the coffee table. She was wearing a pair of knee-high black boots and a denim miniskirt that was about two inches too short, along with a black leather jacket and a T-shirt that said Fresh Cherry Pie, Served Good and Hot. That was Gina's idea of extreme subtlety.

"Boots off my coffee table. I eat there, you know."

"Oh, sorry," Gina said, but her feet remained planted, which was one of the many reasons Nicole would have never let any of her sisters crash at her place after their inevitable divorces or separations. "Why don't you eat at the dining room table?"

"What? Alone?"

"My point exactly. You need to get yourself a man before you reach your old age and have nothing to show for it but a gun collection."

"And what would be so bad about that? I like guns."

Okay, so Nicole said that just to piss off her sister, and as always, it worked.

"You are one sorry-ass little chica if that's what you think life is all about."

Nicole and her sisters were half-Mexican—on their father's side—and half-white, but they'd grown up with their white mother, whose temper had sent their father fleeing when Nicole was two. Yet, Gina insisted on peppering her speech with the limited Spanish words she knew as her way of playing up her minority side and playing down her white-girl side. Strange how no one ever thought it was cool to be a white girl.

"So what? You think I should live by your example instead and go get myself a new man every time something in my life goes wrong? Have three kids by three different fathers, and every time *Jerry Springer* comes on it'll be about something that's happened to me?"

Nicole didn't wait for an answer because she already knew what Gina would say. Instead, she spun around and headed for her bedroom to pack.

"You little bitch!" her sister called out as she flipped through a magazine, the pages slapping together with each flip.

That was her standard answer any time she had no immediate comeback. She'd think of something in a minute and come storming back to the bedroom to argue some more.

Nicole had to admit, she kind of missed this part of having her sisters around. It was sick that she actually liked to argue, but she did. It was probably a by-product of having grown up with three sisters. Arguing had been a way of life in their house.

She found a duffel bag under her bed, then started filling it with underwear, pajamas, a few changes of clothes, her toiletries…. She paused in the middle of placing her cosmetics bag in the side compartment. She was packing as if she was going to be staying at a friend's house, but was she?

Would she really be able to resist Ethan? Sure, she felt as though she could now, but whenever she got near him, there was that *thing*.

That vibe.

Could she resist? Or should she be packing the jumbo box of condoms, all her best panties and her sexy pj's with the see-through top and the lace bottoms?

No, that would be way too obvious. She grabbed her red flannel pajamas out of the bag, inspected them for wear and tear, and decided they were a little tired-looking. Then she went hunting for the new pink satin pj's her mother had given her last Christmas that she hadn't worn but a few times because she didn't care much for pink. For whatever reason, a sleepover at a guy's house—even a guy she really didn't want to sleep with—seemed to call for hot pink satin pj's. A little sexy, but not too revealing.

Dear Lord, she was losing her mind. Any respectable person would have stuck with the red flannel or maybe a T-shirt and some boxers, but Nicole clearly had a bit of Arroyo family blood in her that she couldn't shake no matter how much she tried.

Just in case, for the sake of common sense, she went into the bathroom and grabbed the box of condoms she kept hidden under a towel in the cabinet, then peered out of the bathroom hoping the coast was clear to make it back to her bag. But there stood Gina, with her impeccably bad timing, and her gaze dropped immediately to the condom box.

Damn it.

Why it bothered Nicole for her sister to know she had an active sex life—in theory, anyway—she couldn't say.

"Just a friend? Does your friend need rubbers?"

"I always keep protection with me. Just in case," Nicole said lamely, heading back to her bag.

"You are so full of shit. Why can't you just admit you're going to get laid? What's so bad about that?"

"I don't want to discuss my sex life."

"You're not lying about not being a virgin, are you? Because if you are, that's just really, really sad."

"Why would it be sad if I were saving myself for…marriage, or whatever people save themselves for these days?"

"Oh, God, can you imagine, not even knowing if a guy is good in bed before you marry him? How awful would that be?"

She looked at Gina and narrowed her eyes. "You've really got your priorities straight, haven't you? I mean, that whole good-in-bed filter's really worked out well for you over the course of…what? How many marriages and countless failed relationships?"

Nicole dropped the box of condoms in the bag, covered it with some clothes, and then realized it was possible Ethan would go through her bag when she wasn't looking. What would he think? He'd be convinced she had every intention of sleeping with him, even though she didn't, and if she didn't, why the hell was she packing the condoms?

Gina was fuming, glaring at Nicole so hard she could feel the look burning into her forehead. "At least I *get* laid. At least I know how to have a good time, instead of always being an uptight prude who can't uncross her legs without worrying about a breeze penetrating her panties."

"Oh, sure, hit me where it hurts," Nicole deadpanned, but her gut did give a little lurch at the *uptight prude* accusation.

Was that how the whole world saw her? Was that what she really was? In all her efforts to stay in control and not lose herself to the wrong guy, had she turned into a caricature of a woman?

Well, at least no one could have accused her of being a prude Friday night.

She went to her lingerie drawer, pulled out her sexiest panties and matching bras, along with a black baby-doll nightie she'd never worn, brought them to the bag and dropped them on top of the pile of clothes inside. She cast a look at her sister, daring her to comment.

"Be sure to take the store tags off those before you try to seduce anyone in them," Gina said.

"Screw you," Nicole shot back as she zipped up the bag.

"Oh, and the skinny part of the thong goes in the back, in case you haven't worn one before."

Nicole tried not to laugh but failed. When Gina saw that she'd gotten to her, she laughed and flopped down on the bed, then lay back with her arms over her head. Her shirt slid up, revealing a little C-section scar on her belly from her third baby, Tyson, who tried to come out breech.

"I know how to wear a thong, thanks."

"Don't look at my scar, bitch." Gina paused, and then said, "You ever going to have any babies?"

A question their mother asked approximately once every three months. She must have thought asking over and over would eventually get her the answer she wanted.

"I'd have to actually have a father in mind to help produce the hypothetical babies, but…" Nicole sighed.

Did she want babies? She had no idea. She was happy enough playing auntie to her many nieces and nephews. She saw how much work parenthood was, and she loved her own job enough that she never wanted to give it up, even for a few years.

"But what? You're afraid of getting screwed over by some jerk guy? The babies are still worth putting up with the assholes—just to get the kids, you know?"

"That's a charming way to look at it."

"Shit," Gina said, shrugging. "Life happens. You can't avoid having fun forever out of some silly fear that you might get hurt or things might get messy."

"You're definitely the expert on messy."

"Messy is where all the fun is."

Nicole frowned and remembered she hadn't packed any extra shoes. The last thing she needed was philosophy from Gina. But that's exactly what she was getting, and it really pissed her off that her sister's uninvited words of wisdom weren't sounding so dumb right now.

Her life may have been controlled and she may have had a successful career thus far, but she did feel a little...hollow. Or something. Maybe not hollow in the sense of wanting a baby, or hollow in the sense that her career didn't fulfill her—it did—but maybe hollow in the sense that it would be nice to have someone to share her life with.

"I'll keep that in mind next time you call me crying about your latest breakup. In fact, I'll make a note of it next to my phone and repeat that very slogan to you, okay?"

"I don't expect you to understand it at all, so spare me the advice. I might have had some pretty crappy breakups, but at least I'm happy with my life and I don't have any psychopath murderer guys stalking me."

"I'm happy with my life too!" But why was Nicole suddenly feeling so defensive about it, if that was true?

Was it because Gina's logic rang with a little note of unexpected truth? Had to be it. Nothing more. Really.

"Sure you are."

"I really need to go, okay? Is there any reason you stopped by other than to harass me?"

"Mom wants me to get the real scoop on all this stalker shit. You're not going to let her worry endlessly and drive the rest of us insane, are you?"

"That pretty much sounds like my plan. I mean, no matter what I say, she's going to worry endlessly, right?"

"Why'd you even tell her about all this stuff?"

"I didn't want you guys stopping by here to visit me while I'm gone and risk being followed…or worse. I need to make sure I don't have to worry about you being in danger too."

Gina sat bolt upright on the bed and looked as if she was about to throttle someone, namely, Nicole. "And you let me come here to your place? You put me in danger? Why didn't you warn me? We have to get the hell out of here!"

She was scrambling off the bed, when Nicole grabbed her by the arm and said, "Calm down. There's a cop outside keeping an eye on things here, and the guy who's after me knows it. He's not going to come looking for me in broad daylight with a cop right there."

"How do you know? It happens all the time in the suspense novels I read. Just when some dumb-ass thinks they're safe, that's when the killer is actually watching or getting ready to come after them."

"That's fiction. This is real life, in case you haven't noticed lately."

Nicole grabbed the bag from her bed and carried it to the living room, then set it down in front of the door. She glanced around the apartment, trying to think of what she might be forgetting. She didn't want to have to come back here again, not until Pulatski was caught.

"Yeah, well, real life's a hell of a lot stranger than fiction. If you get me killed—"

"Stop it, Gina. I'll follow you home and make sure no one else is following you. Will that make you feel better?"

"That's the very least you can do," her sister said, pouting now.

They left the apartment, and Nicole locked the door, her pulse racing at the thought of going back to Ethan's house. Going back to temptation.

Could she handle it? Could she stay in control?

Did she even want to?

What she really wanted, she feared, was to lose control once more, to take all her pent-up desires and burn them up with Ethan for a little while. All the explosive chemistry between them would be a nice stress relief, an escape from harsh reality. Unfortunately, this was a time she needed to stay on alert, to look out for dangers.

And here she was worried about condoms and sleepwear.

She needed to get a grip.

10

ETHAN LOOKED OUT the front window at the empty yard and tried to imagine danger lurking there. All he could picture though was Lou, the guy who did the yard work, and he was no threat. But then Nicole's car appeared in the driveway again, and Ethan's heart lurched in his chest.

She'd come back. She'd told him she would but he hadn't quite believed it. Maybe she'd left something here at the house, or maybe she wanted to give him a good kick in the family jewels, or maybe she had some other unexciting reason to be here, but none of those thoughts quelled his excitement.

She was here. That's what mattered.

He watched her park, get out of the car, and head toward the front door.

Stupidly he glanced down at himself to make sure he was dressed now. Of course he was. With a death grip on his repositioned towel, he'd gone straight from the curb to the bedroom—cursing himself the whole way—and put on his clothes before he incited someone to arrest him for indecent exposure. Of all the humiliations he'd ever suffered, the ones that occurred in front of Nicole were the ones that bugged him most.

The rest, no big deal. He could laugh at his own asinine behavior most of the time, but Nicole made him want to rise above his own inadequacies and be more...something. More impressive. Less flawed. Something like that.

He flopped down on the sofa so as to appear as if he hadn't just been watching out the window, but when the doorbell rang, he realized it didn't matter anyway. It wasn't as though she could see inside the house. But he could just tell her to come in, and then she'd see him being all casual and aloof, right? Didn't women like aloof?

"Come in," he called out.

He heard her turn the doorknob, then push the front door open. She stood there looking around the room until her gaze landed on him.

He realized seconds too late his mistake—an unlocked door.

"Are you out of your freaking mind?" she said by way of greeting.

"I saw you through the window. It's not like I was inviting in a stranger."

"The door, Ethan. You didn't have your door locked!"

"I could say I unlocked it when you pulled up, but...I'd be lying," he admitted sheepishly.

She closed the offending door and pointed to the knob. "You see this little thing here? It's called a lock. You turn it, and it keeps bad people out."

"Ha ha. I'm not amused."

"Do you have a death wish?"

"No, I was just so sure you'd come back I wanted to make it easy for you to get in, in case I wasn't able to rush to the door to greet you."

She made a show of locking the second dead bolt on the door, then latching the security chain. "You're lucky I didn't send you a rent-a-cop."

"You're standing in my living room again—there's no end to my good fortune."

"I'm not going to sleep with you, no matter how charming you think you are."

Ethan noticed for the first time that Nicole had a duffel bag slung over her shoulder. Which just went to show how distracted he always was by her finer attributes. The full curves of her hips, the delicious weight of her breasts, the sexy mystery of her eyes.

Those eyes. Those delicious brown eyes that reminded him of velvet, of chocolate confections.

Those eyes that were looking at him as if he were some bit of crap stuck to the bottom of her shoe right now.

"That's cool. I mean, I'm glad you decided to stay, and…I'm sorry for that vulgar thing I said earlier."

"Which one?" she asked, and he couldn't tell if she was dicking him around or serious, or both.

"Of course we don't have to sleep together for you to stay here. That's all I meant. I mean, unless you want to sleep with me, and that would be perfectly nice too, but—" He stopped abruptly, aware too late of his own stupidity.

"You really have a way with the ladies, don't you? Who knew you were such a smooth operator?" Her tone, flat and sarcastic, matched her facial expression, and Ethan couldn't help but laugh.

"Stick around. I'm sure I'll continue to impress with my astounding tools of seduction."

He got up from the couch and closed the distance between them, curious to see if she'd become any less hostile in close proximity to him. He reached out as if to take her bag, but she didn't offer it, so instead he said, "I'll show you where you can put that down in the extra bedroom."

Which was really his second office. God knew why he felt like he needed to have two of them—one for work and one for personal stuff—but he did. He suddenly wished he'd bothered to clean up the mess of papers on his desk. And then there was the bathroom.

Dear God. This being an old house, there was only one bath, and Ethan wasn't exactly Mr. Clean. He made a mental note to sneak into the bathroom ASAP to give it a thorough scrubbing.

"How will you work from home if I'm taking up your office space?"

"No big deal. I have a laptop computer I can work on, and the dining room is my official at-home work space. What about you? Don't you have to work during the day?"

"I've been put on temporary furlough for the next week or so."

The closer they got to each other, the harder it was to think of anything but Nicole. He became hyper-aware of her body, of the soft candy scent that emanated from her. He had no idea what perfume she wore that smelled so simultaneously tempting and sweet, but whatever it was, it was his new favorite scent.

His whole being seemed to focus in on her. He ached in all the usual places, but he ached in some new places too. Indefinable places. As if his body *and* soul ached for her.

This was what happened when he had really great sex. His brain got all mucked up by it and he started thinking about souls and true love and stuff. Which was probably why he'd never had a successful relationship of more than a year or two, max.

That fact worried him. Was he defective? Was he so sex-obsessed he was doomed never to be able to think straight about women for whom he had sexual feelings?

Ethan led Nicole into the bedroom and began converting the couch out into a bed. "I'll have to find some linens. Sorry it's not already set up."

"No big deal. I can do all that. What's important now is that we go over some safety ground rules for the interim until Pulatski is caught, okay?"

Ethan stopped once he had the bed unfolded and nodded. "Sure. Can I get you something to drink? A beer maybe?"

He took a step closer to her, curious again to see if it would have any effect.

"Yeah, that's great. I—" She stopped.

He was only a foot away now, and he could feel the pull of their bodies toward each other. He could feel an increased awareness of everything about her. If he wasn't mistaken, he could even smell the subtle, musky, delicious scent of her, which was impossible. Minutes ago, he could only smell her perfume.

But now, this close… Could it be? Could he really be smelling *that,* when he knew for a fact that he'd never catch the scent otherwise unless he was having sex with her?

His gaze met hers, and he had to have looked like a man in serious need of some action. But he tried to focus on her, on what she might be experiencing. He caught something in her eyes. Longing? Desire? Heat? It sure as hell appeared to be those things to him.

"Are you okay?" he asked.

If he wasn't mistaken, he could see a little film of sweat on her forehead. And he wanted to pull her close and lick it off.

That would not have gone over well, he was quite sure.

"Um…yeah. It's weird. I just feel a little flushed or something."

"Let's get you that beer," he said. But he couldn't look away from her. He was riveted to that spot, riveted to her eyes, her presence, her body.

"Yeah, let's." But she didn't move either.

Ethan's dick was fully rigid now, rock-hard and throbbing for Nicole. The scent had done it. Or maybe her proximity, or the images of having sex with her that kept flashing in his head.

All of it. And him, rock-hard.

"Do you…um…" How to say it? How to ask a woman who'd just as soon kick him in the balls as kiss him if she felt the same irresistible sexual attraction that he did? "Feel like there's some kind of…um—"

"Magnetic pull?" she said. "Like if we get too close we can't help but, um…"

"Have sex," they said simultaneously.

His cock did a victory dance.

"Yeah," he said. "I feel it. I'm not sure I could move away from you right now if I tried."

She reached up and wiped the perspiration from her forehead. "Me either."

"So…" he said, wanting, as he'd never wanted anything in his life, to pull her to him and kiss her, strip off her clothes and taste her mouth, her neck, her breasts, her belly, her hot, wet pussy. Bury his cock in her and never leave that spot.

From somewhere below, a little song began to play in a high-pitched tone. Nicole's cell phone, apparently.

The disruption knocked her out of her daze. She reached for the phone, and answered it, stepping away from him as she did. Farther and farther away, until she was in the hallway and he was standing bereft of her presence by the fold-out couch.

"I told you," he could hear her saying in a put-out tone. "I'll be at a friend's house, and no, I'm not going to give you the phone number or address. That would only put you in danger."

Ethan willed himself to move. He left the room and went in the opposite direction from Nicole to the kitchen, where he retrieved two bottles of Corona, popped the tops, and carried them to the living room. While he waited for her to finish the call, he took a long deep drink of beer and tried to clear his mind of sexual thoughts.

Which was sort of like trying to remove the green from a frog. It couldn't be done. And why the hell did beer make him think of sex too? Probably because half his romantic encounters had involved it.

"Yeah," Nicole was saying from the hallway. "I promise I'll call the minute there's any news. Okay, goodbye."

She came into the living room, looking annoyed rather than aroused. Damn it.

"Who was that?"

"My sister. She's the family snoop assigned to getting every detail of my life on the run so she can spread the news around to everyone."

"I'm sure they're all just worried about you. You have a big family?"

"Humongous. Three sisters and countless nieces and nephews. And those are just the family members I'm in contact with regularly."

"No kidding—I've got three sisters too. Mine are mostly back in London and the suburbs of the city. Can't say I miss the meddling."

Nicole picked up her beer and took a long drink. The sight of it brought his erection back instantly. Beer bottles were so phallic, so sexy when held in the hand of a beautiful woman.

And he wanted to see her nursing his cock the way she nursed that beer. Over and over until he came in her mouth, or on her breasts, or her belly. Or he'd hold off and come inside her, his favorite spot to end a glorious round of sex.

By some stroke of luck, he'd forgotten to clear off the second sofa in the room, leaving the space beside him the sole place for her to sit. She took a seat next to him and looked rather uncomfortable, sitting there not knowing what to do with him when they weren't having sex.

But she'd inadvertently created that proximity thing again. Or was it inadvertent?

The magnetic pull was there. In full force, and when she looked over at him, he knew she felt it again too. He knew, praise heaven, she wanted him. And by the look in her eyes, it was in a bad way.

_11_

NICOLE WASN'T SURE she'd ever forgive herself for sitting on the couch next to Ethan. For one thing, she'd known it would make her get that crazy, dizzy, out-of-control feeling again. And for another, she'd known that if she got that close to him, there'd be no resisting the next step, and the next, and the next, until they were down and dirty on the floor, using up her box of condoms.

And in spite of all her good sense, all her self-control, she'd also known deep down that what she really wanted was to lose control again. To experience that irresistible feeling of all her willpower slipping away, letting herself be pulled toward him.

Losing control. It was the most seductive urge in the world to her at that moment. And she could not turn away from it.

Her gaze landed on the photo of the smiling women she'd seen earlier. Grateful for the possible distraction, she pointed at it and said, "Are those your sisters?"

"Yes, and my mum."

"Are you close to them?"

"Sure. We're not in touch as much as we used to be now that I'm here in the States, but I try to make it back for the holidays whenever I can. And they all nag me via e-mail about when I'm going to settle down and have a bunch of brats, whenever they get the chance."

"Sounds familiar—about the kids I mean."

"Yeah? You're a career girl, must drive your mother batty that you haven't settled down yet."

"You'd think my sisters and their ridiculous number of kids would be enough."

"You feel like you're missing out on anything?"

"No, not at all," Nicole said, hoping it sounded more genuine to Ethan than it did to her.

She really didn't long for the kind of conventional life most people did. She'd always dreamed of having a life of service, doing something that contributed to the greater good, and she was living out that dream. She liked being able to throw herself into her work completely without feeling any guilt that she was neglecting other parts of her life.

Because, basically, there were no other parts. Okay, there were her friends, and they were pretty low-maintenance. All she had to do was show up for Friday-night girls' night and they were happy. But she was beginning to miss not having someone who cared if she ever came home from work or not.

"Yeah, me either," Ethan said. "I'm not sure if I even got the settling-down gene."

"I hope it's not something we inherit—otherwise I'm doomed, judging by my family."

"My father definitely didn't have it. He was a first-class scoundrel."

"Was he around when you were growing up?"

"On and off. He fooled around on my mum throughout their whole marriage, always had a mistress or two on the side and wasn't very good at lying about it. He'd disappear for weeks or months at a time, then show up again like nothing was wrong, until my mum finally got sick of his ass and threw him out for good when I was eleven."

"Oh jeez, I'm sorry. That must have been rough on everyone."

"Mainly on my mum, I guess. She raised us on her own mostly. By the time I was old enough to know what was going on, I got kind of obsessed with tracking down clues about my dad's activities."

"So those were your earliest journalistic efforts?"

"Pretty much, except I didn't write up a story on any of it—I just stored the information away in my head and developed anxiety disorders worrying on my mother's behalf."

Nicole shook her head, thinking of her own absent father and struggling mother. "You and I have more in common than I thought."

"Your dad wasn't around either?"

"My mom scared him away. She has that effect on

men, and I can't say I blame them for running off. She means well, but she's kind of a nutcase."

"Aren't we all?"

She smiled. "Yeah, good point."

"I feel like everything I do is a reaction against my father, which is pretty nutty when you come right down to it."

"Maybe not, if it helps you figure out how to live your life the right way. Does it?"

"Maybe. Or else it makes me terrified of ever making any of his mistakes. Committing to someone before I'm ready, that kind of thing."

"So you're one of those commitment-phobes, eh?" Nicole didn't mean to pry with the question, but it did sound that way. She herself was probably as commitment-phobic as the next person, given her track record.

"I guess you could call it that. I'd never want to do to anyone what my father did to my mum, and really, he didn't seem like such an awful guy on the surface. He just found out too late, I guess, that he wasn't suited for the married with kids thing."

"It's scary, isn't it? Trying to figure out what you're supposed to do with yourself, once you've got the career thing figured out?"

Ethan nodded. "Yep. One wrong move and lives are ruined."

"Or maybe we're just too cautious. Too busy trying to control everything. Well, I am anyway."

"Ah, yet another way we're alike. Mutual control freaks."

"You? A control freak? Come on."

"It's true. I hide it beneath this impossibly charming exterior purely for the sake of getting laid, but it's there."

Nicole laughed. After the way he'd acted earlier, trying to lay down the ground rules about sleeping together, she could actually believe it. "I prefer to think of myself as a mild Type A personality."

"Oh?"

"It's probably the reason I ended up a detective. Makes me feel like I have some kind of control over the chaos in the world."

"There's nothing mild about you, darling."

"Stop trying to be so suave," she said, but there wasn't much force behind it. She had to admit, once she relaxed a little with Ethan, she couldn't help but be taken in by him. He had the irresistible ability to laugh at himself and the world around him.

"You think growing up with a single mum made you want to be the woman in charge?" he asked.

Nicole had never thought about it that way, but maybe there was some truth to it. "I guess I subconsciously wanted to be the opposite of my mother," she said, then winced. "Ugh, sorry. There's nothing worse than listening to me sit around trying to psychoanalyze myself."

His blue eyes sparked with their usual cool charm,

and Nicole felt herself melting again. "I could listen to you read grocery lists in Chinese and find it utterly fascinating."

Her responses to him were becoming so tiresomely predictable, she wanted to kick some sense into herself. But then her gaze dropped to his mouth, and she imagined the feel of it on her, the heat of his kiss, and her female parts flushed with heat.

She took a long drink of beer to steady herself, then set the bottle down on the coffee table. Ethan was watching her so intently, she wondered if he'd developed X-ray vision in the past minute.

They'd been talking about something only seconds ago, but she suddenly couldn't remember the topic. So instead of scrambling to come up with something to say, she did what her entire body was aching to do. She leaned over and kissed Ethan.

The heat that had flooded her breasts and panties spread throughout her body now, and at the contact of his lips on hers, she sighed into his mouth. She felt her pulse quicken, her breath whooshing out of her, a vague dizziness overcoming her brain. She could think of nothing but his physical presence as he pushed her back on the couch and pressed his body on top of hers.

When she felt his erection against her crotch, she could think of nothing else but having him inside her. Right now. Immediately.

Such pulsing, aching, wanting. Such an unbelievable

intensity. She'd never felt anything like this before Friday night. Never wanted to feel anything else but this.

She'd lost her freaking mind.

Somewhere from deep in her consciousness, a little voice of reason screamed, "Stop" and Nicole pushed against Ethan until he got off her.

"What's wrong?" he asked, breathless.

"What the hell is wrong with *us?* It's like we've gone insane. I said no sex, and nearly the first thing we do when we sit next to each other is start going at it hot and heavy."

Ethan shrugged. "We're two healthy adults with physical needs. It's pretty natural. It's just the way of nature—"

"I don't need a biology lesson. We have to stop it."

"I don't mean to sound dense, but is there any particular reason why?"

"Because I don't want to have that kind of relationship with you. Because I don't believe in sex for the sake of sex. And most importantly, because there could be a crazed killer stalking us, and we need to keep ourselves focused on that and not on getting laid every five minutes."

"How about just once a day then?" he said, smiling, but she couldn't summon the good humor to smile back.

She was angry at him, angry at herself, angry at the world.

She hated losing control more than anything else. And yet she hated how seductive it was too.

"Seriously, Ethan. We need to establish some ground rules. No touching, no flirting, no sexual stuff at all. Do you understand me?"

"Absolutely."

He moved away from her on the couch, sat as far away as he could get, and she should have been happy. She should have breathed a sigh of relief. But instead, she just felt miserable. Totally freaking miserable.

<u>12</u>

ETHAN SPENT the rest of Sunday and most of Monday trying his damnedest to avoid getting too close to Nicole. He'd felt such a connection with her when they'd finally let down their guards and talked openly, that he was terrified now of screwing it up with more sexual advances or anything else that might piss her off.

She was a hot-tempered thing, that was for sure, and he admired her fire, probably because he had the same passion within himself, though it usually stayed hidden by what most people took as his affable British exterior. While her passion spilled out all over the place, whether she realized it or not, his was channeled into his work.

He was having a hell of a time focusing on work with Nicole bumping around his house, jamming dowel rods in windowsills and installing extra locks.

Ethan's editor had made it clear that he needed to wrap up his research of the Jonas Pulatski story soon, while it was still news that he was out of jail. But now there was this whole other angle to consider—that

Jonas was out to get Nicole and it seemed him, too—and that pretty much blew his original story idea out of the water. How could he objectively write about a man who apparently wanted to kill him?

He couldn't. And he needed to let his editor know about his predicament, except he found the story utterly fascinating and didn't really want to give it up. Okay, what probably fascinated him most about it was that Nicole was involved.

Spending the past twenty-four hours cooped up in his house with her was enough to leave him itching for something to focus his mental energy on besides figuring out how to get her in bed again, so he'd been reviewing his notes on the Pulatski story, drafting his article, in spite of the fact that he shouldn't have been writing it at all. Bizarrely, it was yet another way for him to focus on Nicole, while still feeling vaguely productive at the same time.

As if she'd sensed him trying his damnedest not to think about her, she came wandering into the room humming what sounded like a Donna Summer song.

"Whatcha' working on?"

"My story on Pulatski, although I should probably be handing it over to someone else right now."

She stood behind him and read the text on his computer screen, which made him crazy. "I really prefer not to let anyone read my rough drafts," he said, then minimized the document before facing her.

"It read almost like you were glorifying what Pulatski did."

"Look, it was a rough draft—a shitty one at that—and the article isn't going to be published anyway. My editor gets word of the fact that Jonas is out to get me and she'll pull the story."

"And then you'll try to sell it elsewhere, or why would you even be writing it?"

"To be honest, I was writing it purely as a distraction from you."

She crossed her arms over her chest and narrowed her eyes. She was probably taking his statement as an insult, but if he explained that he just found her too damn interesting and sexy to have in his house without being distracted, she'd get pissed about that too. It was a lose-lose situation.

"You can't write a story that glorifies a killer, especially not one as awful as Pulatski," Nicole said, and Ethan could nearly feel the fury emanating from her.

"I have no intention of glorifying him or what he's done. I just want to explore his life and his crimes, as a profile of how a normal kid evolves into a hardened killer. What's so wrong with that?"

"Because it's the kind of story that's all about selling newspapers and has nothing to do with telling people anything they need to know."

"I think people do need to know what breeds a

criminal and how the criminal mind works. Knowledge is never a bad thing."

"If it helps further the cult of celebrity around guys like Pulatski, it is. It gives other criminals something to aspire to, and it's an insult to the victims to do any kind of article that shines the light away from their story and onto the perpetrator's."

"You've got a pretty narrow view of the issue, if that's what you really believe. We're going to have to agree to disagree here."

"Hey, since you very well could be his next victim, you go ahead and disagree with me. No problem. Then you won't even have to worry about researching or writing the story."

"Could you be something besides hostile for a few minutes?"

She glowered harder at him now, not saying a word but still communicating plenty.

"Nicole, listen to me. I am perfectly willing to consider other angles on the story. You could even be the subject of it, frankly. That is, if you were willing."

"Me?" she said as if he'd just suggested she take a job at a topless bar.

"Sure, if I went at it from the angle of how it feels to be the cop left behind, the one who witnessed Pulatski's last crime before he went to prison. What lasting effect that's had, and then spin off into a bit of background about him and his other crimes."

He knew it was a long shot Nicole would agree to any such thing, and judging by her still-stiff posture, he was right. She hated the idea.

"Not a chance," she finally said.

"Why not? Afraid of developing your own cult of celebrity?"

"It never happens to the people fighting the criminals, only to the scumbag murderers."

"Why do you think that is?"

"Because people are dumb asses."

He could have argued with her, but he found himself utterly charmed by the simplicity of her conviction. Stopped dead in his tracks by how strongly she opposed what he wanted to do. She had the power to do that to him, stop him in his tracks anytime, anywhere, about anything. It was amazing, really. No one else could wield such power, especially where his work was concerned.

"If you feel that strongly about it…"

"Don't let me stop you from writing your crap story," she said, all mock-casual.

"You mean the one that I really have no intention of publishing now anyway? I really can't win with you on this one, can I?"

She said nothing, just glared.

"Maybe I *should* write it and send it out, just to tick you off. It's pretty fun to watch you get angry."

Ethan tapped his pen against the desk, and Nicole

glanced down at the noise and made a face at the offending object.

"You keep reminding me that I hate journalists."

"Thanks."

"You're all angling for something. The stories you report are never the straight truth. It's always just one person's version of it, complete with a political slant."

"Isn't that the case about everything? I mean, is it within the realm of possibility for humans to have an unvarnished view of the truth, regardless of subject matter? We can try, but we can't really know for sure."

"What have you been smoking? Nothing illegal, I hope. In case you haven't noticed, the truth is the truth. Everything else is a lie."

"It's not that black and white. I believe in reporting the truth as much as anybody," Ethan said, gearing up for his favorite rant. He'd spent more than a little time considering the nature of Truth with a capital *T*. "We see everything through the filter of our own experience, which distorts the truth as we see it. There is some greater sense of truth out there with regard to objective matters, but within our experience, it's all subjective."

She looked at him as if he'd just killed a puppy. "You are so wrong."

"Then we'll agree to disagree."

She sighed and stormed off, and Ethan glared at his computer, frustrated by all the sexual tension in the house, frustrated by having Nicole so close and yet emotionally so far.

He had to get out for a little while. Take a breather, get some distance from the angry whirlwind ball of sexual energy named Nicole Arroyo.

She might not be keen on him leaving, but that was her problem. He'd go anyway, maybe even sneak out and leave a note so he wouldn't have to deal with another argument.

And his plan would have worked if she hadn't caught him trying to slip out the front door with his laptop tucked under his arm.

"Where are you going?" she asked.

"Oh, um, nowhere really. Just outside to work."

She raised her eyebrows, clearly not buying his story.

"Wherever you're going, I'm going too."

Oh, bloody hell.

"Fine, I'm going to my office to gather some work files."

"I'll drive you," she said, and Ethan thought about arguing but decided against it.

He actually did enjoy her company. Even her argumentative nature, which he found fun and incredibly stimulating. It was the frustration of trying to keep sex out of the mix—sex, an essential part of how they needed to relate to each other—that was driving him batty.

The two rode in awkward silence most of the way

to the newspaper offices, with an alternative rock radio station turned up loudly enough to keep them from having to talk. Finally Nicole reached out and turned the station down, then cleared her throat.

"I should apologize," she said. "I've been a bitch, and I'm sorry. You're the most respectable journalist I know, and you didn't deserve my bad attitude earlier, nor did you deserve my meddling in your work."

"Hey, it's okay. This situation, being cooped up worrying about some killer out there waiting for us, is bound to create some tension."

"I think the tension is as much about my reaction to you as anything."

"Oh?" Now they were getting somewhere. A ridiculous little flutter of excitement rose up in Ethan's belly.

"I mentioned already that I get caught up in the need to feel in control of things, and especially in control of myself. But when I'm around you, I start feeling like I'm losing it—losing control, I mean."

"Yeah, I know that feeling all too well."

"And we can't blame it all on that damn lust potion either, even if it does turn out to have some narcotic effect."

"Because it's always been a little out of control when we get together, hasn't it?"

"In my limited experience, yes," she said, and Ethan wondered for the first time just how experienced Nicole really was.

He'd always assumed she was just as bedroom-savvy as the next girl, but...

"Limited experience?"

"Well, I just meant you and I haven't been together except for a few times, and—"

"What about you and other guys? Are there many?"

"How the hell is that any of your business?"

"It isn't. I'm sorry. I was just curious. I mean, we hang out in similar circles, and I've never seen you around with anyone."

She sighed. "I haven't been around the block that many times, if that's what you're wondering. I've had a few sort-of-serious relationships, a few not-so-serious ones, and that's about it."

"A woman as gorgeous and passionate as you should have been around the block more than a few times by now, you know."

"I grew up watching my mom's rotating selection of men do her in, and now my sisters are suffering a similar fate, and I just don't want that to happen to me. I'm waiting for the right guy to come along before I give away the farm."

Ethan tried not to smile. "You've got a whole farm in those tight jeans of yours? I'm impressed."

"Shut up."

Okay, okay, it was a cliché to call a Latina woman fiery, but the word fit Nicole so damn well. He got a hard-on when she said something as simple as *shut up*.

"You know, if you ever give up looking for Mr. Right and want to settle for Mr. Right Now, I'd love to take you around the block a few more times—or fifty, or a hundred. You know, just for the sake of experience and all."

He pinned his gaze solidly on the road, hoping it would force her to subconsciously do the same and not try to hit him while she was driving.

"How generous of you, Ethan."

"But let's get back to these intense feelings I evoke in you. Could you describe that a little more?"

She laughed. "God, you're insufferable."

Outside the car window, the busy freeway exit gave way to palm-tree-lined streets, a bridge over the waterway, and then the route toward downtown. San Diego was a city of ocean and beaches and hillsides, of blue skies and laid-back people. A far cry from gray, cold London. As much as he loved the city where he'd been raised, it was occasionally difficult to imagine living there again after having spent years in California.

"Do you think that we're just such kindred spirits, we can't help but get aroused by each other?"

"I never would have called us kindred spirits before, but the more I get to know you, the more I think you might be onto something there. You had me fooled with that whole charming British-guy act."

"It's taken me years to perfect it."

"You think the real you can't get laid or something? Is that it?"

Ethan was silent for a moment, mulling over her question. "You know, I think it's a case of us being kindred spirits. Just like you're terrified of turning into your mom, I feel the same about my dad."

"How does pretending to be easygoing keep you from turning into him?"

"It's more like, if I never get serious, I don't have to worry about any woman getting serious about me, right?"

He glanced over at Nicole, and she shrugged. "Makes an odd kind of sense, I guess."

The part he didn't feel comfortable speaking up about, the part he wasn't sure he wanted Nicole to know, was that he feared he *was* like his dad in some of the most important ways. He feared he'd never want to settle down with one woman.

Although…

If he were going to settle down, he could almost imagine doing it with a woman like Nicole. Someone who excited him and challenged him and kept him on his toes.

When they reached their destination, Nicole said she'd wait in the lobby while he went in to take care of business.

Walking into the newspaper offices never failed to give Ethan a little jolt of adrenaline. Chasing down sources, seeking out little-known details, putting all the pieces together to form a cohesive whole fuelled his intellect. His insatiable curiosity led him on quests for answers. As a result, he'd never once dreaded coming to the office.

He sat down at his desk and tried to remember everything he needed to grab to take home.

"Where have you been?"

Ethan looked up in the direction of the female voice that had asked the question, and found Kathryn leaning over his desk.

"Hey, Kat. I've been sitting right here at my desk. Why?" For the past five seconds, anyway.

"I meant this morning. You were mysteriously absent, and no one knew why, but there was this big rumor circulating about a crazed murderer on your trail."

Ethan winced. "Yeah, well, the rumor is fact, I'm afraid to say. I just came in to gather some files to work on at home."

Kathryn's eyes widened. "Dear God, Ethan. Are you going to be okay?"

He nodded toward the reception area where Nicole was pacing back and forth, her arms crossed over her chest, her eagle eyes scanning the premises for dangers.

"I've got all three of *Charlie's Angels* rolled into one out there covering me. I think I'll be fine."

Kathryn followed his gaze. "Is that the cop you used to have the hots for?"

"Still have the hots for, to be honest." He thought about mentioning the spilled lust potion and the wild sex that had followed, but it felt like kissing and telling, and if there was one way Ethan was strictly old-fashioned, that was it. He never talked about the intimate details of his love life, except to his lovers.

"Oh?"

"Don't think you're going to drag any lurid gossip out of me."

"Do you really think I'd spread office gossip?"

"No, I know you're above it, but I'm still not going to spill any details, other than to confirm that yes, Nicole is acting as my twenty-four-hour-a-day personal bodyguard, and it's a hell of a burden, let me tell you."

"I'll bet." She flashed a brilliant smile. "So did you get any word about that fake lust potion stuff from the crime lab?"

"Wish I could say I have, but no. They were pretty backed up so might not have the results back to us for weeks."

Zoe appeared beside Kathryn, having just escaped what was probably a tedious editorial meeting. "Results of what?"

"That lust potion stuff."

"Oh, right. Rumor has it you were behaving like a man with a serious case of lust on the dance floor at La Casa Friday night. Any truth to that?"

"God, you're good."

"That's why they pay me the big bucks," Zoe said. "It's my job to find the gossip and report it, so watch out, you keep behaving like you did and you could show up in my column."

"I doubt your gossip column audience is sitting on the edges of their seats waiting to hear about my love life. Don't you?"

"You never know. It's a good story—handsome man-about-town reporter, mysterious Latin beauty, a nearly obscene encounter on the dance floor followed by a hurried exit to parts unknown but easily guessed…"

Just then, she spotted Nicole outside. "Speaking of Latin beauties, who's that?" Zoe's keen gaze pinned Ethan, and he could tell she was putting two and two together and coming up with the answer to her own question.

"That would be the woman from the dance floor incident," Kathryn offered. "At least, that's an educated guess on my part."

Zoe's mouth gaped open. "She's so enthralled with you that she's pacing outside the office while you work? You must be good! You've been holding out on us."

"There's no way to sound appropriately modest and talk about what a great lover I am at the same time."

"Okay, what's she really doing out there?" Zoe asked.

"She's his bodyguard," Kathryn offered oh so help-fully.

"Oh." Zoe instantly went smug. "A bodyguard with privileges?"

"You're pushing your luck, Aberdeen," Ethan warned.

"If I hadn't known any better, when I heard the rumors about you and the salsa club, I'd have thought you'd swigged down some of that lust potion and let it go to your head. So to speak," she said.

"What about you two? There's no reason to stand around talking about my love life when we could be talking about yours."

"Don't try to divert attention from yourself," Kathryn said, sounding suspiciously uncomfortable with his attempt to change the subject.

But he knew better than to push Kathryn. She was one tough cookie who only talked about herself in her own good time. If she wanted anyone to know anything, she'd tell them.

Zoe cast a mysterious glance in Kathryn's direction, that her friend didn't seem to catch. Something was probably going on in Kathryn's private life, whether she wanted to admit it or not.

"Listen up you two," Ethan said, glancing down at the stack of files he was about to take home with him. "I'm going to be working from home for the immediate future, so if you need to get in touch with me, you can catch me on my home phone, my cell or e-mail."

"I didn't know we had the work-from-home option now," Zoe said.

"We don't, exactly," Ethan answered. "It's more like, there's some crazed killer stalking me and it's not safe for me to stick with my usual patterns of going to work and so on. The police are afraid I could be endangering my co-workers if I show up here."

"So that rumor's true too!" Zoe said in shock. "Oh, gosh, Ethan, I'm so sorry. I thought that one was way too outlandish to be believed."

"You're telling me."

"Who is this guy and what does he want with you?"

"He's a former cop killer just released from prison. Unfortunately, I made the mistake of contacting him for an interview, as I was thinking of doing a follow-up story on him, but then he apparently spotted me with Nicole—" he nodded at her out in the lobby "—and the nutcase decided I'd be his next target along with her. Apparently he dislikes cops and the reporters who sleep with them."

"Please let us know if you need anything," Kathryn said. "I'm so sorry you have to deal with this crap. Why do they let creeps like that back out on the street, anyway?"

"To make San Diego a happier place," Zoe dead-panned, rolling her eyes at the nonsensical nature of the justice system, which they'd bemoaned many a time while discussing cases Ethan had covered, a dizzying number of which were committed by repeat offenders and ex-convicts.

"Don't you girls worry about me. I'll be fine with Miss Commando out there looking after me. But if I get any out-of-control fantasies to act out a ménage à quatre—"

"Ew," Zoe said, wincing. "Four just seems like a bad number for those kinds of arrangements."

"So does three," added Kathryn.

"Yeah, actually, you're right. I don't know how the ménage à trois gained such popularity anyway. There's always bound to be an odd man—or woman—out, right?" Zoe said.

"I'm perfectly happy to give it a go if you are," Ethan said, all mock-casual.

"Don't even think about it," Kathryn warned.

"Well, you can think about it, just not while I'm around," Zoe said. "And I don't want to know what you're thinking."

"Guess I'd better get out of here before my bodyguard comes and physically removes me from the premises."

"Send us updates if you have the time, okay? Let us know you're doing all right," Kathryn said.

Ethan nodded, and each woman gave him a hug in turn.

While he sometimes joked around with them about a sexual attraction, the truth was they'd become much more than potential conquests to him. He preferred to stay away from office romances, but office friendships such as the ones he had with Zoe and Kathryn were priceless. They were the kinds of friends he knew he really could rely upon when times were tough. If he'd asked them, they probably would have taken shifts acting as his bodyguard themselves.

He chuckled at the image when they left his desk, gathered his files in a box, and headed for his editor's office to explain the Pulatski situation in more detail.

Karen Wyman had become almost like a surrogate mother to him since he'd taken the job at the *Times*. She wasn't exactly the nurturing type, but she was always available with a listening ear and good advice when he needed it. He knocked on the door to her office, which stood a little ajar, and then pushed it open when she called, "Come in."

Karen glanced up from some papers and smiled when she saw him. "I'm so glad to see you here in one piece. What's the latest on this ex-convict you mentioned on the phone?"

"Nothing to tell yet," he said, sitting in the visitor's chair across from her.

"So what's up?" she said, setting the papers aside and giving him her full attention. "You know you're approved to work from home for as long as you need to, right?"

"Sure. Remember that story on Jonas Pulatski I've been researching?"

She nodded.

"I'm not going to be able to do it now, because Pulatski's the ex-con who's apparently out to get me."

"Oh, Ethan, I'm sorry. I know how much work you've put into the research. It's a shame you won't get to write the story."

Her reaction was exactly as he'd expected—she'd pulled the plug. Although he hated to drop a story unfinished, a part of him was relieved to have the matter taken out of his hands. "I'm not sure what his problem with me is. But given the situation, I don't see how I could write the piece objectively now."

Karen eyed him speculatively. "If anyone can do it objectively, I know you can. But that's a moot point since you're not on the story anymore."

"I'd be happy to pass my research on to someone else here at the office if you'd like." The questing, curious side of him still wanted to see the article taken to completion, even if he wasn't the one to do it.

She shook her head. "Let's just let this whole thing die down. I'm concerned about your safety first. The story is a distant second."

"I'll keep you updated on how things are going and when I think I can get back to the office."

"Take your time," she said as Ethan rose from his seat and edged toward the door.

They said their goodbyes, and he hurried through the main office trying to avoid making eye contact. He didn't feel like explaining his situation to every other person he passed, and he was feeling guilty for keeping Nicole waiting so long. When he reached the door to the lobby, he could see Nicole still pacing back and forth, looking impatient.

"Hey, sorry that took a bit longer than I expected," he said when he entered the lobby.

Nicole shrugged. "Yeah, well, you seemed to be having a good time chitchatting."

"I was just saying goodbye to a few friends," he said, surprised by the tone of her voice. "Are you okay?"

They walked to the front door of the building and exited, then headed toward Nicole's car.

"I'm fine," she said stiffly.

"Are you jealous of me talking to two attractive women?" he said, unable to contain his smile at the thought that Nicole would give a rat's ass one way or the other.

She shot him a deadly look that said exactly how stupid he was to even mention the *j* word.

The sky outside was a bright crystalline blue that occurred on days like this when the humidity was low and the breeze was brisk. Overhead, palm trees rustled in the light wind, and the chill in the air made Ethan wish he'd worn a jacket the way Nicole had. Only the natives ever seemed to know exactly how to dress for San Diego weather on any given day. The key seemed to involve layers of some sort.

"You can't possibly be serious," she finally said. "Me? Get jealous over you? Why?"

He shrugged and pretended to give the matter some

thought. "Because of my impressive bedroom skills? Perhaps they're so impressive you can't bear the thought of any woman but you benefiting from them?"

"Were you smoking something at your desk in there?"

He made a wounded face. "Oh, that hurts."

"You asked for it."

"Come on now. I couldn't have been the only one enjoying myself when we were together. Seriously. On a scale from one to ten, one being 'you might as well have gone to sleep' and ten being 'the best sex of your life', where do I rate?"

She laughed then, and it was a sound so rare Ethan almost thought she was faking it. But no, her laugh seemed genuine. "Haven't I already answered this question, or some similar version of it?"

"I don't think I ever proposed a rating system."

"Okay, then, if you really want an answer, I'd rate you a…4.5."

Ethan stopped in his tracks, and Nicole didn't notice it until she'd continued down the sidewalk another twenty feet or so. She finally stopped, turned around, and glared at him for a moment before coming back.

"You wound me," he said.

"You totally set yourself up for that. What kind of guy asks for a number rating?"

"I bet we all would if we thought we could guarantee the right answer."

"And you were so sure of yourself you figured the answer would be an automatic ten?"

He shrugged and started walking slowly again. "I thought I'd rate at least an 8.5, maybe a 9.5 if you were really being honest."

She laughed again, and he couldn't help smiling at his own audacity. He wasn't serious, of course, but he loved goading her.

"So how would you rate me?"

"Definitely a 4.5, no doubt."

"Oh sure. Say that now."

"Well, what kind of woman asks for a number rating, anyway?"

"Okay, I walked right into that."

"Was I really that bland? Below average even? Come on, be honest. For the sake of my future lovers, I need to know so I can work on improving myself."

"Oh, really?"

"I'll embark on a vigorous sexual self-improvement program, with daily practice. You could even be my instructor in the process."

"Right. Keep on dreaming."

"But I forgot—you're the inexperienced one, right? So maybe you haven't had enough good lovers to compare me to, to know how fabulous I really am."

"Yeah, maybe it's like judging a sports competition. I don't want to give away the high scores too early and risk finding someone who'll blow my whole rating system out of the water in a few years."

"Or maybe with the way you're stomping on my manhood, I'll never be able to get it up with a woman again and will be relegated to getting myself off by hand for the rest of my life. Would that make you happy?"

"You're a guy. That's not a very likely scenario."

"What? You think your words aren't crushing my ego right now?"

They reached the car, and Nicole opened the trunk for him to set his box of papers inside. Once it was in place, he got in the car.

When she got in too, she answered, "I think no matter how crushed your ego might momentarily get, it will always spring right back up to superhuman-sized proportions and will never in a million years get in the way of your enjoying sex."

"Want to test out that theory? My schedule's all clear this afternoon. We could see what else pops back up besides my ego."

She rolled her eyes at him and started the car, then pulled out into traffic heading north. "We're not sleeping together again."

"That's what you keep saying, and somehow we keep rolling around on the floor together."

"I was a little pent-up, that's all. I'm over it now."

"If I'm only a 4.5, you must be more than a little pent-up to keep sleeping with me. Hard up is more like it."

She slammed on the brakes, thrusting Ethan against the seat belt, which pinched at his collar bone and nearly knocked the breath out of him. He looked up to see that they'd reached a red light, and she'd apparently only stopped short to make a point to him.

"For a cop, you're kind of a lousy driver."

"I'm not hard up."

"Then why do you keep sleeping with me?"

"It's only happened three times. I'll make sure it doesn't happen again," she said, glaring up at the stoplight.

"You *are* hard up—that's the problem, isn't it? I was right when I guessed that you don't even have many lovers to compare me to so you're picking 4.5 to be safe. You know, to leave room for higher rankings in the future."

"Dream on, Ethan. Dream on."

Ethan was growing to love their sparring. He suspected Nicole did too. He had forgotten how much he loved a good argument, having grown up with a houseful of sisters.

"It must be impossible to have much of a sex life working in the environment you do, with all those macho men around just dying to prove you're only a woman, not worthy of working in their ranks."

The light turned, and she stepped on the gas a little too hard, throwing him back against the seat.

"It has its challenges, and yeah, there's definitely

no room for letting my guard down on the job, especially about personal issues."

"I'm sorry. Men can be such assholes."

She cut her gaze to him then stared straight ahead at the road again. "Is that your standard ploy? To act like the enlightened male appalled at the behavior of your brethren?"

"Is it working?"

"Not really. You'd have to actually have some enlightened actions to back up the talk before I could believe it."

"Damn it, there's always a catch."

She laughed finally, a little more relaxed. "I guess I might have been a tiny bit harsh with the rating."

"I knew it! Now tell me my real rating. 8.6? 9.4?"

"Um…5.2."

"That's rubbish! I demand a recount."

Ethan was seriously starting to feel insecure. He reviewed their encounters in his head. Her reactions to him, her enthusiasm, how wet she had gotten, how visibly excited she'd been, the number of times she'd come. It all added up to either her being incredibly sex-starved, or him being a much better lover than she was willing to admit, or maybe a combination of both.

Regardless, he fully intended to find a way to improve his score with her. Soon. Very soon.

13

"DO YOU HAVE ANY IDEA how to defend yourself against an attacker?" Nicole asked.

"You mean with karate or something? No." Ethan shook his head.

The two stood facing each other in his dining room-slash-office area, where there was enough floor space that they could practice some self-defense moves and roll around on the floor a little without anyone getting their head bashed in by a piece of furniture. It had taken two days of Nicole's nagging and a bunch of mysterious hang-up phone calls to convince Ethan that he needed to swallow his male pride and actually learn a little about self-defense.

It wasn't exactly a hardship having Nicole as his instructor, but it was a bit humiliating to have it demonstrated without a doubt that she could kick his ass if she really wanted to.

"Not karate, just generally. As in, what do you do if someone tries to attack you?"

"Duck and run?" he said, smiling, still not quite able to take this whole thing seriously.

The hang-up phone calls could have been some teenagers playing a practical joke, or maybe the kids next door who'd gotten the eyeful of his package a few days ago.

"That's sure to impress the ladies," Nicole said, unable to resist smiling at his bad joke.

He did love that he could get to her that way on occasion.

"I pride myself on my ability to impress the ladies, as you know all too well," Ethan said casually, and an image of the night they'd spent together two years ago invaded his head. He'd tried hard to block it out, had considered his failure something best put behind him and not examined too closely.

If he couldn't get it up, regardless of being drunk, he was partly to blame. It hadn't been just the alcohol, he knew. It had been him, maybe unable to perform when it counted most. He'd never let himself admit how profoundly attracted to Nicole he was, and how much it meant to him to be able to impress her. But now, getting to know her better, spending more time with her, he knew she was like no other woman he'd ever known and no other woman he would ever know in the future.

She was everything he'd always wanted in one perfect package. But it wasn't fair to want her so much, when he couldn't promise forever, was it? Or was it okay, since she clearly didn't want a lot to do with him anyway? It was Wednesday, and she'd been staying at his house for only three days, but already he was feeling such a profound ache for her, he didn't think he could take another night of having her in his house without having her in his bed.

"Is this how you protect yourself, by being completely oblivious to security issues?"

Ethan shrugged. "I didn't think I needed to get my panties in a wad. This is a decent neighborhood."

"You're a crime reporter, for God's sake. You know crimes happen here just like anywhere."

"I guess reporting on that stuff all the time kind of makes me numb to it. I start thinking it's a normal part of life and don't get paranoid about any of it."

"That's about the most ass-backward thing I've ever heard."

He surveyed her head to toe, standing in the middle of his dining room poised as if she wanted to kick his ass. He wasn't sure whether to be intimidated or turned-on. Well, turned-on was a given, but it struck him then how arousing intimidation could be. Maybe that's one of the thousand things he found attractive about Nicole—that she was one of the few women he'd met who he was quite sure could take him down if she wanted to.

"Okay, okay. You're right. I need to be more careful, especially now that we've got Mr. Psycho stalking us."

"Whatever you do, don't take this lightly," she

said, her expression stern, unwilling to lighten up even for a second.

"You can be a real hard-ass, you know," Ethan said, unwilling to totally submit to her agenda.

Nothing was quite as fun as watching Nicole get mad. No, wait, that wasn't true. Making love to her was a hell of a lot more fun, but aside from sex acts…

"Yeah, I think we've covered that already. Are you even listening to me?" she said.

"Of course I am."

"What did I just say?"

"Um…"

"You were staring at my crotch the whole time I was talking."

Oh shit. Okay, so maybe he'd missed something.

"I apologize. It's just that I find your, ah, female regions very distracting."

He watched her expression transform from pissed to outraged. This was the disadvantage of being a guy—the ability to say the absolute stupidest thing at the absolute worst time. *Brilliant, Ethan. Just brilliant.* It might be fun to watch her get angry, but it definitely wasn't going to be fun to feel the toe of her shoe slam into his forehead.

But before she could give him the thrashing he deserved, the phone rang. Again. A trace had been placed on his phone, but so far the calls had all come from the few remaining pay phones in the area. Which made the idea of the calls being kids pulling pranks unlikely, but still, Ethan figured it was possible.

Or not.

He watched Nicole's expression harden, and she went to answer the phone.

"Hello?" she said into the receiver. "Hello? Who is this? Can you please tell me who this is?"

A pause.

"Who are you? Jonas? You know we're going to catch you, don't you?"

A second later Ethan could hear a dial tone even from where he stood across the room, and then Nicole replaced the receiver on the desk.

When she turned back to him, she looked a little pale.

"He said something this time?"

"He told me to check the back patio, that there's a present there for me."

"What the hell? How could he have gotten back there unnoticed?"

Nicole shook her head. "I don't know. He's trying to make fools of us."

She peered out the patio door, standing to the side a bit using the wall to shield her body. Ethan came up behind her and looked out too. At first glance, nothing appeared different. But after a few moments, he spotted a doll's head poking out from the ivy vines on the fence next to the patio.

"Right there," he said, pointing.

Nicole's gaze darted down to the spot he indicated, and she reached for the cell phone at her hip. She called in a report about the call and the evidence waiting outside, and once she finished, she put the phone away and eased the door open.

Closer now, Ethan could see that this doll was male, and it had brown hair like his. It was covered in a red substance that looked eerily like blood, and the same substance also stained the patio.

"Nice," he muttered.

"Let's just leave it for the evidence team. I'm not in the mood to deal with this shit right now." She turned away from the doll, and Ethan had to step out of her way for her to enter the house again.

He followed her inside, wishing there was something he could say or do to make her feel at ease. But there wasn't anything. He felt lame and helpless, until he watched her sink onto the couch and realized the best gift he could give her right now was a distraction.

Ethan crossed the room and sat beside her. "I guess this means the self-defense lesson is done for today?"

She sighed. "We'll try again later, or tomorrow, okay?"

"Want to give me a good punch in the nose? Beat on me a little to relieve some stress?"

"That's not such a bad idea...."

"When I first came to the U.S., I became fixated on women's kickboxing matches for a short while. I had a college roommate who attended them and dragged me along, and—"

"What does that have to do with anything?"

"I was getting to the point. I just meant to illustrate that I am not immune to the charms of a woman who knows how to kick ass."

"So you'd get a hard-on if I beat you up?"

He winced. "Maybe not. I'd like to think I could hold my own in a match with you. I mean, what I lack in technical skill, I make up for in brute strength. Plus I've got fifty or sixty pounds on you, easy."

She made an effort to smile, but it faded fast. "I'm sorry. I can't be much fun to be around right now. I just hate this trapped animal feeling that goes along with sitting around waiting for Jonas like this."

"Maybe he'll have tripped up this time. You never know what piece of evidence will be the one that leads the police to him."

"I should be out there on the job, not sitting here like a victim."

"But you are on the job protecting me."

"Whole lot of good I'm doing. The asshole managed to walk right up and put that doll on your patio without anyone—including me—seeing him."

"Don't be too hard on yourself, Nicole. You can't have eyes in the back of your head."

Her mouth was so soft, so lush, it was difficult not to kiss it whenever he looked at it. But right now would have been an incredibly bad time for a kiss, he sensed. Or maybe it wouldn't have. He was wallowing in indecision when Nicole asked, "Why did you move to the U.S., anyway?"

"For college. I was chosen for an exchange program at USC, and after that I got the job here at the *Times* and moved to San Diego."

"And you're here for good?"

Ethan nodded. "It took me a while but I came to love it here, so I applied for my citizenship after graduating."

"Is it weird leaving your home country for good?"

He smiled. "Have you ever tasted English food? Or lived through a London winter?"

"Come on, you must miss your family and friends from back home."

"That's what air travel is for."

"Yeah, I wouldn't mind having my family separated from me by a nice long plane ride sometimes."

"Eventually it felt like my home was here. I don't regret a thing." And he never regretted being as far as possible from the tired, bitter dynamic between his mum and his no-good father.

Nicole opened her mouth to say something, but the sound of a car door slamming out front distracted her. They stood and looked out the window to see a police cruiser parked in the driveway, along with a second unmarked car pulling up behind.

"I'd better go out and talk to them," she said. "But I'll take a rain check on that distraction, okay?"

Ethan was pleasantly surprised by her playful smirk.

"Any time," he said.

"Thanks for trying to cheer me up. It really did help," she said over her shoulder as she headed for the front door.

Ethan watched, let his gaze drop to the delicious curves of her ass in a pair of white yoga pants. His usual aching for her—the physical desire for her that was so constant he'd already come to accept it as a normal part of his life—was accompanied by another ache, this one deeper, centered somewhere he couldn't pinpoint. He simply ached for her company, her companionship, her engagement. And already, watching her walk away felt like a loss.

NICOLE HAD NO IDEA how to ease the frustration of being with Ethan without sleeping with him. After three days cooped up with him and a second near-disastrous self-defense lesson that nearly ended with her stripping her clothes off and mounting him right there on the floor, she knew something had to give.

The close quarters of his tiny house were feeling closer by the second, and her only escape seemed to be the privacy of the bathroom. And the lure of the removable showerhead, which, while it wasn't a live male, and definitely wasn't Ethan, was at least a serviceable substitute that could relieve some of her frustration.

Sometimes, being a woman who loved sex too much to allow herself to have it much really, really sucked.

And okay, so she'd lied about his sexual skill level. What was she supposed to say? That he was by far the best lover she'd ever had? That the chemistry between them was so intense, all she had to do was think of him and she was instantly wet and ready? Yeah, that would cement their professional relationship big-time.

When they'd finished the self-defense lesson, she'd tried distracting herself with television, then with a book, then with pacing around the house under the guise of looking for security breaches. None of which helped. All she could think about was sex. With Ethan. ASAP.

So she told him she needed a shower and disappeared into the bathroom. She undressed and turned the water to near-scalding, then got in and washed up. It was only after the tension built to a near boiling-point that she allowed the showerhead to dip between her legs. She was still sudsy there, still slippery, and she massaged herself with one hand while directing the water spray with the other.

The intense sensation was almost too much to take, but she pressed herself against the shower wall and forced herself to take it. She needed the intensity. She needed the outlet, fast and simple. She slipped two fingers inside her hot, slick opening and moved them in and out while letting the spray massage her clit, and in no time, her body was quaking, and her breath quick.

She was about to come when she heard the bathroom door open. Nicole gasped and dropped the showerhead, then hurried to pick it up.

"What are you doing? I'm in here!" she called out.

Instead of answering, Ethan pushed aside the shower curtain and peered in at her.

"You look amazing," he said.

"Get out," she said, but he didn't budge.

"I just couldn't pass up the chance to see you all wet, even if you won't let me touch you."

"Why the hell won't your bathroom door lock?" She glared at him and tried to pull the curtain closed again, but he held tight.

"Precisely for opportunities like this."

"Get out of here now!"

"I'd like to point out first though that my sexual skills are heightened in the shower. I'm at least an eight in this particular setting. Wouldn't you like to have an eight?"

Nicole aimed the showerhead at him full blast, and he was instantly soaked, his light blue oxford shirt clinging nicely to his chest and his jeans sporting a huge dark blue spot on the front. He sputtered and tried to grab it from her, but she dodged his grasp and sprayed him again.

"Get the hell out or you'll be even more soaked, along with the rest of your bathroom."

Instead of obeying, he started taking his clothes off. "I'm all about water conservation," he said. "I believe in communal showering."

She should have sprayed him again, or kicked him hard in the balls, but her body was still tense with her interrupted release, and she was desperately, wildly horny.

Seeing Ethan all wet with his shirt off now didn't help matters. Not one little bit.

Okay, so she had no willpower. So she was prone to screwing him whenever he got within three feet of her. There had to be an explanation. Maybe she could blame the lust potion after all. In which case, she could enjoy him without feeling too guilty. She could bask in the best sex of her life for just a little while longer until the potion's effects dissipated.

By the time Ethan had his pants and boxers off, she was pulling him into the tub, and when he pressed his erection against her abdomen and kissed her hard, she moaned into his mouth, grasped his hips with both hands, and pulled him harder against her.

She wanted him inside her right that second. No teasing, no foreplay, just screwing. Right now, up against the shower wall.

"I want you now," she demanded.

And he obliged, as always. He lifted her leg and propped it on the edge of the tub, bent his knees a little, produced an already-open condom from the shower caddy, positioned his cock between her legs, and slid into her all the way, where she was so wet, he didn't encounter even the slightest resistance.

"You were getting yourself off in here, weren't you? That's why you're already so wet and your nipples are standing up like that," he said as he pinched one lightly between his fingertips.

He watched her with a half-lidded gaze as he moved slowly inside her and played with each of her nipples. He couldn't have seen anything on her face but unabashed, out-of-control lust.

"So what if I was?" she said between gasps as he pumped into her, pushing her precariously close to orgasm again.

A half smile curved his mouth. "I just want to know if you've been violating my showerhead. What rating does it get, by the way? A 3.7?"

"No, you've definitely been outdone by the showerhead," she dared to joke.

He stilled inside her, narrowed his eyes, and tried his best to look offended. "Is that so? Maybe I should let you get back to your real lover then?"

She was beginning to see that one of the things that attracted her most to Ethan was that he essentially wouldn't let her push him around. Sure, he'd act as though he was a big pushover on the surface, but whenever she really tried to push him, he stood strong. He wasn't intimidated by her.

Which was a huge turn-on. She'd never met a guy before who could stand his ground with her.

"No!" she said too quickly. "I mean, you know, so long as you're here." She glanced down at their bodies joined together and smiled an apologetic smile.

"Tell me my real rating," he said. "I know you were lying earlier."

"And what if I wasn't?"

"You wouldn't want me here unless you were lying. You didn't exactly fight me off, you know."

"I still could."

"But you won't."

She sighed. "No, I won't."

"Because?"

"Look, the no-sex thing was a bad idea, okay? I admit it!"

"Oh?"

"As long as I'm here, we can have sex."

"I'm still waiting to hear my real number," he said, a devilish smile playing on his lips.

The feel of him inside her was too delicious, too much satisfaction to resist. "You're a ten, Ethan. A solid ten."

"That's more like it." He started pumping his hips more urgently now, and Nicole held on to him, kissed him, clung to him because she was too limp with pleasure to do anything else.

Then he stilled and withdrew from her for a moment, turned her around, and let her brace herself against the shower wall again as he eased into her from behind. In this position, he could penetrate even deeper, and she moaned at the heightened sensation of having him so far inside her.

She grasped the towel bar to steady herself more as he moved faster, and her gasps echoed throughout the bathroom. The showerhead still dangled, spraying oddly at their shins, but neither of them were disposed to stop and deal with the thing now, not when they were possessed by something that felt so good, so right.

Nicole felt an odd mingling of sexual relief and a vague sense of dread. But dread about what? She was hardly in a state to be contemplating such big questions, but when she thought of how out of control she felt right now, she knew in an instant. Ethan threatened her every feeling of safety and security that came with being in control.

He turned her world on its ear and made her question why she felt so strongly that she needed to be always controlled, always denying her passions. Sometimes—like right now—it was damn good to follow her passion.

When Ethan reached around and teased her clit with his fingertips, all coherent thoughts vanished. Nicole sank into the sensation, until she felt herself giving in to the orgasm that she'd been on the cusp of all this time. It had been building strength, and it rocked her hard when it came.

She heard herself cursing and moaning and breathing hard as the uncontrollable pleasure wracked her body, and when it was finally done, she wondered how would she ever deny herself such pleasure again?

14

SOMEWHERE ALONG THE WAY, the potion's so-called magic must have turned into real magic. Ethan had no idea what the stuff was, and it wasn't exactly the crime lab's first priority in spite of Nicole's having tried to put a rush on it—they were claiming a six-week backup at the moment on non-urgent jobs—but he didn't need scientific proof to know that it had had some power over them.

It had been enough to get Nicole to give in to him, at least. And that was a lot.

Ethan became aware that he was lying awake in the dark, and he glanced at the clock to see that it was half past three in the morning. Nicole's leg was warm against his, so he moved closer to her, until the length of his body was pressed against hers. His cock stirred, then grew fully rigid and pressed into her hip, but she didn't wake.

Yeah, somewhere along the way, the potion had worn off, but the animal attraction remained. Intensified. Expanded, until the intensity between them was greater than anything they'd experienced initially, under the influence of…whatever that stuff had been.

He tried to imagine explaining to anyone that he'd been operating under the influence of a mysterious lust potion, and he immediately nixed the idea. No one would believe him. He wasn't even sure he believed it himself. But how else to explain that Nicole, with her steel will, had finally given in to him? There simply was no other explanation.

Unless… Unless she'd really been attracted to him all along, and it was just finally their time to be together.

Okay, no doubt it was finally their time, but he couldn't help wondering how long the fun would last. He wasn't the kind of guy to take things seriously, and Nicole knew that. He wasn't the type who could be counted on to settle down, marry, have kids, do the conventional thing, and yet that was probably exactly the kind of guy Nicole wanted. The kind every woman wanted.

In fact, now that they'd had their fun, he was surprised he wasn't already glancing at his watch every five minutes, wondering when to take his leave. It always happened that way. There was that initial period of euphoria with a new lover, followed by a brief period of contentment, followed by a series of arguments, followed by a breakup.

Not that he was cynical or anything. He just knew the pattern of his relationships. Sure, some varied a little, some had more of one part and less of another, and some fizzled without much argument at all. Some vanished into thin air as if they had never existed in the first place.

The stillness of the house, punctuated only by Nicole's soft breathing, lulled him, but he couldn't fall back to sleep. Ethan was wide awake now, all too aware that his relationship with Nicole was following none of the usual patterns. Why the fact had never occurred to him before—well, he'd been too busy with crazed killers and frenzied sex to stop and reflect on things much.

Maybe it was the long courtship process that had mucked things up. If one night of botched sex and two years of pining after Nicole could even be called courtship. Maybe all that pent-up desire was taking a while to work itself out between them.

But then, they'd started out with the arguing instead of the euphoria, and now they were slowly settling into intense euphoria with brief periods of bickering. Almost like…like how he supposed a storybook romance might be. If there was nothing but euphoria all the time, it wouldn't have made a very interesting story. Well, the sex parts would be interesting, but the rest would have been a snore to read.

Whereas his relationship with Nicole seemed to be one upheaval after another. Just when he thought he'd be able to savor the euphoria, some crazy thing happened to muck it all up.

But storybook romances weren't any more real than all the typical romances he'd had, and he briefly considered the inevitable breakup in this story. At that thought, his gut clenched, and he felt as though he might be sick. He didn't want to lose Nicole, but he didn't want things to become boring either.

He wanted to remember her this way, all fire and passion and intensity. In fact, if he died right now, he'd be a supremely happy man.

And he knew, when this thing with Jonas Pulatski was settled, he and Nicole would be done too. She'd walk away as soon as she could, because to her, this was a relationship that was all about sex. It was the same for him, he supposed.

He rolled onto his side and slipped his hand across her warm belly. She wasn't wearing any clothes, and his fingertips quickly met up with her pubic hair. He brushed across it gently and dipped his hand between her thighs, then massaged there ever so softly. She immediately grew damp, the way she always did, and she shifted a little in her sleep. Her thighs parted a bit for him, and his erection strained harder against her hip.

He wanted to be inside her, but only when he was sure she was ready. He'd never woken her up with lovemaking before, but he was having a hard time imagining her being offended by the idea.

He increased the intensity of his stroking until she was impossibly slick, all the while watching her face, which remained tranquil in sleep. When he brushed his fingers across her clit, a nearly imperceptible furrow crossed her brow for a second, and when he lingered there, massaging, she sighed and moved her hips ever so slightly again.

There was no more waiting. He had to be inside her then. He moved over her, rested between her legs, then pushed gently inside her. She was tight, but so hot and wet there was little resistance to his cock. When his full length was in her, he moved slowly in and out, partly loving that she was still asleep with him able to take her this way, and partly wanting her to wake up and join him in the experience.

He loved this intimacy that came with taking her even when she wasn't fully aware of it. The delicious sensation of it nearly caused him to shoot too soon, before he'd even had time to savor the sensations properly.

Nicole shifted her legs, spreading them wider for him even as she still slept, and then when he pushed harder into her, she sighed, and her eyes fluttered open.

She seemed to see him without comprehension for a moment. She blinked in the darkness, taking in the sight of his face over hers, becoming fully aware of his lying on her, making love to her, and then without pause she wrapped her legs around his hips and urged him to pump deeper into her.

When he dipped his mouth close to hers, she kissed him as hungrily as she had when they'd been operating under the influence of the lust potion. Her tongue licked at his, and she cupped his face in her hands as if to hold him right where she wanted him. Not that he was going anywhere.

In bed with Nicole, in her arms, it was impossible to want to be anywhere else.

NICOLE HAD NEVER WOKEN up to someone having sex with her before, and while in theory she was sure she would have protested the idea, in practice she found it so arousing she nearly came on the spot. As Ethan moved inside her, she felt herself getting closer and closer to orgasm, without any other stimulation. And she so desperately wanted more of him, wanted to taste him, feel him all over, she couldn't get enough of his mouth. Couldn't get enough of him, period.

"Is this okay?" he murmured against her mouth, and she could almost hear his smile. "That I was in you when you woke up, I mean?"

"Am I acting offended?" she asked, then kissed him again.

"No," he said, breaking the kiss only enough to speak. His lips were still brushing hers. "I couldn't resist. You looked so beautiful lying here in the dark, felt so warm and good…"

"I can't think of anything better to wake up to," she said, then trailed off into a moan as he thrust in deeper again.

"Really?"

"Yeah," she whispered, then kissed him.

It was true. There was nothing better than this. Nothing better than right now. Nothing better than being with Ethan, anytime, any place, doing anything. Not just having sex.

Even in the midst of all this distracting sensation, the thought occurred to her that they'd managed to be incredibly happy together in spite of the Pulatski situation. In spite of their lives being in danger, these days with Ethan had somehow been some of the best of her life.

Perhaps it was actually the danger of the situation that made them so hyperaware of the good things, so able to appreciate them.

Yeah, that had to be it.

And then Ethan flipped her over and settled her on top of him, braced her hips and began thrusting into her again with her straddling him. She could only be in this moment, in these sensations that were blowing her mind, making her want and ache and desire as she never had before.

He quickened the pace, and his own gasps told her he was close to orgasm. She clenched her inner muscles around him, felt the rising tension of her own approaching climax, and then gave in to it. Her body quaked, pleasure rocked her, enveloped her, washed her mind clean of thoughts.

She cried out, insensible sounds that mingled with

Ethan's as he, too, began quaking with release. He spilled into her, and she caught the delicious sensation of his come shooting inside her.

And then she froze. There had been very few times she'd ever experienced that sensation, and even then, only in long-term relationships in which she'd trusted her lover completely and they'd accidentally run out of condoms—and she'd been taking the pill. The rest of the time, she'd always been too paranoid about pregnancy and STDs to take any risks.

Her gaze met Ethan's, and he caught the distress in her eyes.

"What's wrong?" he said, still a little breathless.

"I'm not taking birth control, and you're not wearing a condom."

"Oh, hell," he whispered. "I'm sorry, I got caught up in the moment and totally forgot. I swear, that never happens…."

She pulled away from him and sat on the bed, putting some distance between them as her mind reeled at the implications.

So this was how it happened. This was how she would go from being a responsible woman in complete control of her life to being just another Arroyo woman who'd let her passions screw up everything. She felt her eyes stinging. She was overreacting, but she couldn't help it. She was paralyzed with anger at herself for letting something so stupid happen.

She should have noticed the more intense sensations of having sex with no condom. She should have stopped them from going too far.

"Is it...a bad time of month?" he asked, placing a hand on her thigh.

She pulled her leg away, scrambling to think when she'd had her last period. It had been at least three weeks, maybe closer to four.

"No," she finally said. "I don't think so. I think we're probably safe from an accidental..." She couldn't even say the word. *Pregnancy.*

It wasn't that pregnancy was the end of the world. With the right guy, she could see herself someday maybe having a baby. Or not. But this definitely wasn't the right time, or the right guy, and to think how close she'd come to being a carbon copy of her sisters and her mother terrified her.

"Oh good. And I promise you I'm clean, okay? I had a full physical with blood work about five months ago. I got a clean bill of health. And I haven't put myself in any compromising situations since then...until now," he said, and she could hear the smile in his voice as he tried to lighten things up a bit.

But it wasn't working. "Don't worry," she said. "I'm clean too." Her last checkup had been nearly a year ago, but her sex life, other than the boat guy, hadn't exactly been active in the past year. Dormant like an ancient volcano was more like it.

And then all of a sudden she'd erupted. With disastrous results.

"Look, Nicole. I'm really sorry about my little slip-up, and I promise it won't happen again…unless you want it to. I mean, it did feel incredible to, you know…"

"Yeah, but I'm not on the pill at the moment—I let my prescription lapse for a while and I won't start taking it again for a week or two."

"Hey, I can wait—"

"I'd have to get some kind of protection, and let's face it, our relationship could be over any day now," she blurted without thinking about what she was saying or how it might sound to Ethan's ears.

But it was true. She knew that as soon as Pulatski was caught, there wouldn't be any reason for them to be in each other's lives, and Ethan was definitely not the kind of guy who wanted to take things seriously. He'd made that abundantly clear.

"Oh," he said stiffly. "Well, sure, if that's how you feel. But the offer still stands, you know, just in case."

"Sure." And she wanted to feel him that way again. Desperately wanted it. There was nothing quite as sensual or intimate as the feel of flesh against flesh in that most private region.

But feeling how precariously close to the edge she'd gotten, how dangerous it was to make decisions based on passion, she knew she had to get away from him as fast as she could. She knew their relationship could go no further than this. Right here, right now. It had to be the end of their sexual involvement.

In that instant, she knew it with the heaviest, most miserable kind of certainty.

And somehow, she had to tell him. "Ethan, we can't do this anymore."

"Of course. I'd never want you getting pregnant accidentally. I'll use a condom from now on every single time, okay?"

"No, I mean sex in general. We have to stop it now. I just can't deal with the consequences."

In the shadowy darkness, with the faintest light from a street lamp pouring in through the window, she could see the disappointment on his face. Could sense it in the air between them.

But on this one point, there was no way she could allow herself to back down. No matter whose heart might get bruised. Or even broken.

Had they entered broken heart territory already? So soon? Had they really come to a place already where they could leave permanent scars on each other's lives?

Somehow, Nicole knew they had. She understood more than ever now that whether it be for good or bad, Ethan had the power to rock her world.

15

OF ALL THE SCREW-UPS in his life, Ethan had a good sense that the no-condom thing with Nicole had been the crowning achievement of his failures. She had some kind of weird family-related issue with being in control, never making a mistake, never taking even the slightest risk of getting pregnant.

And he respected her for that. If everyone was so responsible, there would be no unwanted pregnancies in the world. But Nicole seemed a little more hell-bent than anyone else he'd ever been with.

Ethan stared out the window at the brilliant sunshine, and in an instant he knew he couldn't sit inside this damn house brooding for another day. They needed to get out, soak in some rays, get a change of scenery. Surely there could be occasional mental health breaks from their prison.

He'd made some progress in his research on a story his editor had asked him to cover, in spite of having Nicole around driving him to distraction all the time.

And he'd done a decent job of keeping up with his work from home all week.

But being sequestered like this was beginning to feel pretty pointless when there hadn't been the slightest sign of Pulatski in a couple of days, not since the second voodoo doll incident. The police had no leads, other than having discovered that the blood on the doll was from a cow—probably from a local butcher—and there hadn't been so much as a strange bump in the night at his house since the calls stopped. Probably Nicole intimidated even the mice too much for them to come anywhere near.

Behind him, he could hear Nicole sit down on a bar stool, and he turned to find her sipping a cup of coffee. Things had been tense between them since the no-condom incident last night, and while they'd both eventually fallen back to sleep, it had been a fitful rest. Nicole hadn't said a word all morning.

No more sex. That's the last thing she'd told him. She didn't want to make love to him anymore, and he was trying not to take it personally. But the truth was that it felt like a monumental rejection. As though the moment he realized what a great thing they had together, she snatched it away.

It hurt. But what did he expect from a woman who'd spent two solid years putting him off, telling him no? Did he really think it was realistic to expect that all of a sudden she'd give him nothing but yes?

When he took into account their history, it was easy to see that there wasn't much chance for them to last more than the explosive week they'd had. And he was going to have to be happy with what she'd been willing to give him—which was a hell of a lot better than the nothing she'd given him for so long.

He was just pissed at himself for blowing it. He'd accidentally found her Achilles heel—the pregnancy thing—and he'd cut it, thereby screwing things up for himself.

He was, if nothing else, a royal goddamn screwup.

But there was no sense sitting around dwelling on his inadequacies.

"Any chance we could escape the house for the day? Maybe go down to the beach or something just to get out and enjoy the nice weather?"

Nicole took another drink of her coffee before answering. "I'm not sure. I mean, well… I don't see why not. I'll have someone tail us and keep an eye on things wherever we go."

"You're serious? I thought you'd tell me no."

"Sure, let's do it. I'm getting tired of being stuck inside. And I'm beginning to wonder if that voodoo doll thing wasn't just some kind of sick prank pulled by God-knows-who."

"Great," he said. "So let's go."

If he couldn't have sex with Nicole, at least he could go do something else fun with her to keep his mind off what they were missing out on. And the more he was around her, the more he realized how much he did enjoy her company out of bed. When she let down her guard, she was, quite honestly, the most disarming woman he'd ever met.

Now if he could just convince her he wasn't a complete dolt…

Not that it mattered. Good things always came to an end, but he found himself wishing she could be more than his lover. He found himself wanting her as a companion and a friend.

NICOLE COULDN'T REMEMBER the last time she'd been to the beach boardwalk. It was a relief to get out of the house after the tense morning at home with Ethan. She needed the fresh air, the sunshine and the distractions that a change of scenery provided. Anything but more dwelling on her own miserable thoughts. It was Friday already—she'd been staying at Ethan's house for almost a week, and still no progress had been made on the search for Pulatski.

Ethan and she walked together along the open sidewalk that passed amusement park rides, tourist shops and arcades. Nicole wasn't sure why she felt the need to ride the Tilt-A-Whirl at this stage of her life, but when she spotted it, she dragged Ethan to the nearest ticket booth and bought them both a ride.

Maybe it was the way Ethan had gotten her used to

feeling off balance that made her want to go even further with the tilted feelings.

"You can't possibly expect me to ride that bloody thing," Ethan said, looking appalled.

"You can't possibly be afraid of such a tame ride. Are you?" She smiled a teasing smile, and he narrowed his eyes at her.

"Are you taunting me?"

"No. I'm daring you to admit you're a big wuss."

"Okay, I'm a big wuss, and proud of it. Happy now?"

"No, I want to see you ride the ride. I mean, how scary can it be?"

"I get motion sickness, if you must know. So unless you'd like to see the remnants of a toaster waffle splattered all over your lap, you might want to reconsider."

"Jeez, Ethan. You're no fun at all."

The ride stopped, and she stepped into place in line to get on. Alone, apparently. She glanced over at him standing by himself at the railing and felt a tiny bit bad for giving him a hard time.

"I'm sorry. I'll bring Dramamine next time," he said, shrugging.

"You must be a barrel of laughs on a cruise ship," she said right before handing her ticket to the ride operator.

Once she'd found a seat in one of the compartments, she felt immensely stupid to be sitting solitary on a kids' ride. Why had she bothered getting on without Ethan? Because she was stupid and stubborn and wanted to prove something that didn't even matter.

She was about to unbuckle herself and climb out when she felt a hand grasp her arm, and she looked up smiling, expecting to see Ethan. Instead, she saw Jonas Pulatski. Older than when she'd last seen him, maybe a little more hardened around the eyes, but unmistakably him. With his free hand, he held a gun to her side.

"Come with me, and don't make a sound," he said.

Nicole glanced around frantically. She'd stupidly chosen a seat that wasn't visible from where Ethan stood, and the plainclothes cop was nowhere to be seen. She suddenly feared for Ethan's life as much as she feared for hers.

She stood and let Jonas pull her toward the metal railing. "Climb over it," he said, and she did, all while he still held her arm.

Now he had the gun concealed in his jacket pocket, and she knew he could get her all the way out of the park without anyone finding them unless she acted fast.

She didn't have a plan though. She'd let herself get so distracted by her issues with Ethan that she'd stupidly let her guard down. She wasn't even wearing a weapon now, she'd gotten so confident in having another cop watching all the time.

She was profoundly, overwhelmingly stupid. She never should have believed they were safe to move about freely at an amusement park, not now, so close on the heels of the threats and phone calls. Part of her had even suspected luring Jonas out into the open would give the guys doing surveillance a chance to catch him. But Jonas was smarter than that, and she shuddered to even think what that might mean for her. Right here, right now.

The key to staying alive though was to stay calm, and look for opportunities.

"Where are you taking me?" she asked quietly, trying her best to sound relaxed.

She almost did a convincing job of it.

"I'm taking you someplace safe and quiet where we can have a nice visit. I've been waiting for you for a long time, Nicole. We have lots to catch up on."

He'd planned his capture of her eerily well for what must have been a spur-of-the-moment act. He was intelligent and incredibly opportunistic. He'd waited until he could slip her away without Ethan realizing she was gone for a minute or so, and then the route he was taking her by winding between buildings was completely counterintuitive to the way anyone might think they'd be going.

And even if Ethan immediately realized she was missing and found them, he was unarmed. He'd get hurt—or worse—if he approached.

"Did you kill the plainclothes cop?" she forced herself to ask.

"Wouldn't you like to know," Jonas said calmly.

"Actually, I'm not sure I want to know, but I need to know."

"Was he a friend of yours? Maybe someone you've fucked before, just like you're fucking that reporter?"

"You've been watching me closely," she said evenly, glancing around as inconspicuously as she could, looking for any opportunity to get away.

But he had a death grip on her arm, and the gun was aimed right at her side. She didn't doubt he could hit her if she ran—he'd proven himself a keen shot in the past.

People were passing by them without paying the slightest attention to the life-or-death situation subtly unfolding right there, in the middle of everything. That's how it usually was. People were too wrapped up in their own lives to notice what was really going on.

Damn it. She'd been such a fool. She'd broken all the rules she had so carefully followed up until today, and Jonas had been there, ready to pounce. He'd known she would let down her guard sooner or later. He'd known her better than she knew herself, and that, almost more than anything else, pissed her off.

"You have no idea how much I know about you, Nicole. I know what kind of panties you like to wear. I know about your sisters, and your mother, and I could hurt them too if I chose. Such easy targets…"

He was baiting her, she knew, but he'd found one of her weak spots.

"Don't even think about it, you bastard," she spat, and he squeezed her arm tighter.

"Now, now. We both know you're the one I've been waiting for."

Nicole realized he was guiding her toward a door marked Employees Only in the back of a maintenance building, and her throat tightened. They'd almost reached their destination, and despite whatever he'd said about a long talk, she knew he would kill her before he'd let her escape. There would be no escape at all unless she could somehow gain the upper hand, even for a few seconds.

Where was Ethan? He had to have noticed she was gone by now, had to be looking frantically for her, had to be calling 9-1-1. But it would be too late, unless she did something now.

"I'm not surprised you were able to find me," she said to Jonas.

"Don't try the flattery tactic. It's completely transparent," he said evenly, his voice revealing neither malice nor amusement.

"You can't expect me to go down without trying everything possible, right? Wouldn't you be disappointed if I didn't put up a fight?"

"Now you're trying to distract me with conversation. Still transparent, Nicole. Give it up."

They were only a few feet from the building now, and Nicole's pulse kicked into overdrive. She felt cold sweat dripping down her rib cage and down the back of her neck. She was terrified as she never had been before.

No, once before. The first time she'd encountered Jonas Pulatski.

That had been the first time she'd been paralyzed by fear. Her fear had caused the death of another officer. And if she let it seize her again, it would cause her death too.

Her throat tightened as he pressed the gun into her side and led her through the Employees Only door. She fought off the fear, forced herself to breathe in and out, forced herself to believe she could find a way out of this.

But as she stood in the dark cool room and the door slammed shut, followed by the sound of Jonas locking it, her hope began to slip away.

16

THE IMAGE OF THAT goddamn ride spinning around without Nicole on it would be burned into Ethan's consciousness forever. How could he have been so stupid as to let her leave his side even for a second? And where the hell were the police when he needed them?

He frantically scanned the people milling about the area, his heart thudding like mad in his chest, his breath suddenly quick and shallow.

Nicole. He had to find her fast. Where was she? The question echoed over and over in his head. Where was she? Where was she? Where was she?

He took off toward the other side of the rides, the direction she would have had to go in for him not to have seen her, and when he couldn't see the plain-clothes cop anywhere, he broke into a run.

Twenty minutes later, he felt as if he'd searched every square inch of the beach boardwalk area, and he'd given a description of Nicole to the area security, who'd also alerted the police. And he had nothing to do but wander aimlessly, praying he'd somehow stumble upon her safe and sound, perhaps having decided to play an extremely cruel joke on him to prove her point about security.

The fear of her in danger had made something abundantly clear to him, though. He didn't just like Nicole. He wasn't just sexually attracted to her. He was falling in love with her.

And if she came to any harm, he would die a thousand deaths.

Then he felt something collide with the back of his head, and searing pain. And then nothing. Just black.

NICOLE STOOD in the dark room, her breath coming out in shallow little gasps, her heart racing, and for a moment she was paralyzed by her predicament. Paralyzed by fear again. But she would not let that character flaw cause her inaction a second time. What if Jonas was going after Ethan now?

What other explanation was there for him leaving her alone? He could have been going back to his car to get some weapon or equipment he needed to deal with her… Either that, or he wanted Ethan now, too.

She would not stand by a second time and let someone she'd vowed to protect get hurt—or worse. Memories of watching Max Robbins get shot crowded her head, and she felt tears sting her eyes. Then she sprang into action.

Feeling around on the wall near the door, she found

a light switch and turned it on. Under the glow of a fluorescent bulb, she could see the various cans of paint, brushes, brooms, mops, buckets and assorted other junk crammed into the closet around her. She tried the doorknob, knowing it would be locked and yet still having her hope slip a bit at feeling its resistance to being turned.

She grabbed a small paint can from the floor and started banging it against the door, yelling for help as she did so. Over and over for a few minutes, she made as much noise as she could, hoping she'd catch someone's attention. Then she caught sight of a crowbar on a nearby shelf and decided to try her hand at busting out the door, a maneuver that was never as easy in real life as it had seemed in her police academy training years ago.

She continued to call for help as she put all her weight into prying the door lock open, but it did no good. Ten minutes later, her arms ached from the effort and her voice was going hoarse. Someone out there had to be hearing her though.

And where the hell was Jonas? Since he hadn't even restrained her or taped her mouth, she would have thought he'd be smart enough to come back fast. Unless...

Unless he knew the real revenge against her would be to hurt someone she cared about again. To make her live with even more guilt. Maybe this was all about getting her out of the way so he could kill Ethan. It was diabolical, but she couldn't deny what an effective means of revenge it would be.

She cried out even louder now for help, and just when her hope was about to take a nosedive, she heard a key in the lock. A second later, the door swung open, and a security guard stood blinking at her.

"My friend—he's in trouble," Nicole said, stumbling out into the bright sunlight, then looking left and right, scanning the scene desperately for some sign of Ethan.

"You mean the guy who reported you missing? Are you okay, ma'am?"

"I'm fine. His name is Ethan. Ethan Ramsey, and I think the man who locked me in that utility room is going to kill him if we don't find them first."

"We've got police on the scene now, since you were reported missing. I'll call in any information you have if you want to give it to me now."

Nicole spewed out descriptions of both men and all the relevant details she could think of in a matter of seconds as the security guard took notes. And then she took off running, but she didn't know where to go, or whether she would be too late.

"I'm going to go look for them, but I'll need backup," she called over her shoulder. "I'm heading to the beach."

Her instincts told her to go there, but she couldn't

say why. Over the years, she had learned to trust her gut as a detective. When she could hear what it said, she found it was rarely wrong. And five minutes later, when she saw a trail in the sand leading toward the ocean, and saw the lifeless form floating in the surf, she understood what her gut had known without seeing.

"Ethan!" she cried as she ran toward the ocean, her feet sinking in the sand and making it hard to move fast. Overhead, seagulls shrieked, and from the boardwalk, people heard her and took notice finally of the body in the water.

She reached the water's edge and splashed into it, praying that somehow, Ethan was still alive. Praying she hadn't failed in her duty to protect once again. But he was floating facedown, and she could see blood oozing from a gash on his head. Her heart sank as she grasped the back of his jacket and hauled him toward the beach.

Only after she'd dragged him out of the water could she feel the bitterly cold water that had saturated her shoes and pant legs. And it was as if the terror that iced her veins had created the chill, rather than the ocean.

When she had him on his back, she dropped to her knees and started to perform CPR. At the same time she could hear people gathering around them, and the shrill police sirens from a nearby parking lot. She was lost in the rhythm of the CPR though, mouth to mouth, then hands to chest, again and again, so that she barely registered when paramedics arrived and someone gently helped her up and away from Ethan's body.

Still lifeless. Because of her. Again.

At first she didn't realize that the keening sound was coming from her own throat, or that her face was soaked with tears. This was not her, not the Nicole who stayed in control and never lost her cool. This was someone else—the woman she'd tried so hard not to become.

An officer she vaguely recognized was standing beside her now, urging her away from the scene and toward an ambulance parked in the lot next to the beach.

"We just need to have you answer a few questions," he was saying, "And make sure you're okay."

"I'm not going anywhere until I know if he's alive," she said, not budging any farther from Ethan. "Jonas Pulatski," she said, the name like ice on her tongue. "He did it."

"A patrol car caught up with him on the west side of the boardwalk. He's being taken in right now," the officer said, and Nicole felt robbed of any sense of relief she might have had, because Ethan was lying on the beach, maybe dead.

She could not live with the guilt again. Jonas had found her weakness. He had gotten his revenge.

She bit the inside of her cheek and shivered in the ocean breeze, watching, waiting, hoping.

THERE WAS LIGHT, then darkness, then light again. Ethan struggled to open his eyes, but he could only see the fuzzy light and darkness, and he could hear himself moaning. He felt as if he were at the bottom of a murky body of water, trying to swim to the surface.

He finally pried his eyes all the way open and stared at the glaring fluorescent lights above. His head ached, throbbed, felt as if it had been bashed against a brick wall. Fragmented memories flooded his mind of panic and searching, then...nothing.

He became aware of someone's presence beside him, and he looked over to see Nicole. Her face was tight, but immediately softened when their eyes met.

"You're okay," she said, half question and half statement of fact.

He watched her smile slowly, his brain taking in the fact that he was in a hospital bed, in a small white room.

"What happened?" he asked.

"You don't remember?"

"The last thing I remember was looking for you—"

"It was Jonas Pulatski. He hit you with a shovel and dragged you into the ocean. You almost drowned."

He could see emotion in her eyes, intense emotion. Relief maybe? She carried the weight of the world on her shoulders in her duties as a cop, and she probably never would have forgiven herself if any real harm had come to him. He was touched by the fact that she clearly cared.

Ethan lifted his hand up to the spot where the

throbbing at the back of his head was most intense, and he felt a bandage there.

"Don't worry," Nicole said. "They didn't shave your head or anything. It's just a gash they had to sew up and bandage. You'll be good as new in a few weeks."

"Oh good, so I'm not bald. At least not yet, eh?"

"Alive and not bald. You've got your priorities straight," she said, smiling wryly.

Ethan could not think of a single person he'd rather see sitting at his bedside at that moment. Nicole, smiling and warm. Nicole, all his pure and impure fantasies wrapped up into one perfect package. Nicole, the best thing he'd ever seen.

"And not shark bait," he joked, but as soon as the words left his mouth, he remembered how dire the situation had been.

He recalled the paralyzing fear of knowing Nicole was in grave danger, the horror at the thought that he might not be able to save her, the fierce adrenaline rush that had propelled him forward in the desperate minutes before his memory became a black void.

He'd nearly lost her. And he had never been so thankful in his life as he was at that moment, knowing she was alive and well. And so was he. Two miracles for the price of one.

"What happened to you?" he said. "Did he hurt you?"

Her gaze dropped to her hands for a few seconds, then she met his again. "I'm fine," she said. "He locked me in a utility room when he went off to find you, but security found me thanks to you, and I got out."

"Thank God. But why did he leave you alone?"

"I'm thinking you were really his primary target. He wanted revenge—wanted me to suffer—and what better way to do that than to hurt someone he thought I cared about."

She seemed to realize belatedly how her words came out sounding wrong.

"Wow," he muttered.

"I'm sorry, I mean, of course I care about you, but—"

"He thought I was your steady boyfriend or something, right?"

She nodded. "I think so. The police are still questioning him, so we might have the whole story eventually."

"So you rescued me then somehow?"

"Not exactly. I spotted you in the water and dragged you out, but the ambulance crew revived you."

A weight settled on his chest, nearly choked off his breathing, and he felt a stinging in his eyes that had only been there hours before, when he'd first seen that Nicole was in danger.

He was not the kind of guy who got the urge to cry twice in one day. Damn it. He was going off the deep end.

She sighed, and the smile disappeared from her

mouth and her eyes. "I just wanted to stick around until you woke up, to make sure you were okay."

"Oh, um, right," Ethan murmured.

Her expression tightened a bit more, and she stood up from her chair. "I think they're going to keep you here for observation, but you can call me if you need a ride home, okay?"

Okay. Right. Sure. She'd made the offer as if she'd be far from thrilled to put herself out for him now that her job was done.

He flashed an easy smile. "Don't worry. I'll take a cab. I'm sure you'll be happy to hear your work here is done," he said, his voice light.

Because that's what Ethan did when things got heavy. He lightened them up. It was the one thing besides his work for which he could always be counted upon.

He didn't want her to walk away. He wanted her to stay at his side, laugh with him, pass the time with him.

That was clearly not what she wanted though. Above all else, Nicole was a woman with a sense of purpose, and she had no lasting interest in him outside of keeping him safe. She'd made that abundantly clear.

Okay, and maybe he was pouting a bit. He was allowed to do that while lying in a hospital bed with his head all bandaged up, wasn't he?

"Take care," she said, then turned and walked out the door.

When the cold sound of the metal door closing into

its metal frame had finished resonating through his bones, Ethan sighed. His gut twisted, and the weight on his chest grew heavier.

Why did he feel as though his world had just ended, if Nicole was just another brief adventure in his oh so interesting life?

_17_

NICOLE WAS NOT going to cry. Not for a second. She blinked away the stinging sensation in her eyes as she drove out of the hospital parking lot. Her car felt empty without Ethan in the passenger seat, but it was a feeling she'd have to get used to. She was thinking like an idiot, like the kind of lovesick fool women in her family were too prone to being. She had to snap out of it. Be tough. Forget Ethan.

She navigated through traffic until she came to a red light, trying her best to focus on the lyrics of the pop song blaring from the radio. But the words to the song were stupid, made no sense, and she switched off the radio in frustration.

All thoughts led back to Ethan. The guy she had to forget, because he could take nothing seriously.

She was all seriousness and he was all play. To him, her emotions were just a game. To him, her feelings were a toy to be batted about, like a cat and its mouse. He'd won the game, and now he'd move on to the next one.

She was a fool for thinking he could be any different.

Nicole hadn't realized she was driving on autopilot until she looked around and realized she'd passed up the freeway entrance and was headed toward her sister Gina's neighborhood. Her first instinct upon realizing where she was going was to stop the car and go in the other direction, but she forced herself to continue on. She needed to talk to someone, maybe even someone who made her own problems seem miniscule. Gina could always do that for her, if nothing else.

Five minutes later, she pulled up to the curb in front of her sister's mobile home and turned off the car, then sat staring at the green plastic ride-on dinosaur that had been discarded by her niece in the front yard. Next to it on the ground lay a pink ball, a naked Barbie doll, and a big green pair of Incredible Hulk hands that her nephew liked to wear while punching everything within his reach.

And somehow, amid the chaos of little kids and no-good men, Gina still managed to be happy. What did she know that Nicole didn't?

Her sister must have spotted her through the front window, because she came bounding out the door wearing a pair of green house slippers with ripped jeans and a white T-shirt. Concern furrowed her brow. Nicole opened the door to get out of the car, but she couldn't find the energy to do it.

"Are you okay?" Gina asked when she reached the driver's side door. "Did they catch that guy?"

Oh right. That guy. Not Ethan. But Jonas Pulaski. In all the uproar of seeing Ethan nearly die and then recover, Nicole had blocked out thoughts of Jonas and how close she'd come to her own doom at his hands.

In an uncontrollable rush, emotion welled up in her throat and cut off her ability to speak. She nodded instead, blinking again at her stinging eyes.

"Nicole, get out of the car and come inside. You're freaking me out. What happened?"

Nicole allowed her sister to lead her by the hand across the yard, into the trailer, where the sounds of kids playing in the back room created a constant din of giggly noise.

Nicole sat on the couch and took a long, deep breath. Inside she was feeling anything but okay, as if the events of the past day were finally sinking in. She opened her mouth to speak and burst into tears instead.

Nicole hadn't cried in front of any of her sisters since probably middle school, when one of them had dumped purple nail polish all over her favorite jeans. Or something like that. And here she was wracked with sobs, her shoulders shaking, her face crumpled beneath her hands.

"Oh, Nic," Gina said, coming toward her now.

Nicole felt her sister's arms embrace her, smelled the sweet scent of drugstore perfume, and for once she didn't want to pull away. She wanted someone to pat her on the back and tell her everything was going to be okay. For once, Nicole needed a shoulder to cry on.

When the sobs waned to sniffles and she'd stopped shaking, Gina pulled back a bit and brushed the hair away from Nicole's forehead, like the nurturing type she was. She'd had lots of experience with this kind of thing, being a mother of three.

"It's okay," Nicole said, gaining a little more control of herself. She took another deep breath and felt the tension draining from her body. "Pulatski was caught. It's just been kind of a harrowing day catching him is all."

"That asshole didn't do anything to you, did he?"

"I'm fine, really. No harm done. He just scared me is all. He hurt a friend of mine, but he's going to be fine. And it's all done. Nothing more to worry about."

"They're not going to let that bastard out of jail again in two years, are they?"

"This is his third strike, so according to the state of California, so long as he's convicted, he'll never be let out of prison again."

"Thank God," Gina said as she patted Nicole's arm and gazed at her with concerned eyes. "Why don't you stay here for dinner? We can order pizza. You can sleep on the fold-out couch, okay? You shouldn't be alone tonight."

And for once, Nicole didn't want to be. She nodded, surprised to be accepting a night of toddlers crying and constant interruptions, even thankful for the offer. She didn't want to be alone where she could think about how it felt to have Ethan suddenly absent from her life, suddenly absent from her bed.

That's what she got for falling head over heels in lust with someone. That's what happened when she was stupid enough to confuse sex with love. Sex was the thing people walked away from.

She didn't want to think about what tomorrow would be like at all.

WORK WAS HER RESPITE. Nicole could throw herself into her job like no one else she knew, and mostly, it helped her forget about the things she wanted to forget. It helped her forget about her problems, about Ethan, about everything but catching bad guys. When she focused on all the bad shit happening in the city, it made her own problems seem tiny and insignificant.

For the past week since the beach boardwalk incident, she'd insisted on working the night shift, in spite of her supervisor's encouragement to take a bit of time off. She'd countered with the argument that she needed something to keep herself busy and keep from moping around, especially at night when she was prone to feeling lonely. He didn't need to know why.

Stiff wind gusts were sweeping in from the ocean now and then, and the early morning air was heavy with moisture from an approaching storm. Nicole inhaled the ocean scent, but beneath her clothes she felt sticky and tired. She wanted to undress, shower and slip into bed naked, except she couldn't do that now without being reminded of things she'd be better off forgetting.

As she walked up the sidewalk to her building, she could see something on the steps up ahead. A person, or a body, lying face-up on the sidewalk. She came closer, and thought she recognized the long, lean legs clad in denim, the brown suede jacket.... Another step, and her breath caught in her throat.

Ethan. Lying back, his eyes closed, his jaw slack, he looked dead. After everything, all the danger, all the protecting him, and Jonas in jail again, how could it be?

She expelled a strangled cry as she dropped her knees beside him, and that's when she saw his chest moving up and down in a slow, steady rhythm. The sound of her cry sent his eyes fluttering open, and he startled, then sat up.

"Oh, bloody hell, I fell asleep, didn't I?"

"Damn it, Ethan. I thought you were dead. What are you doing here?"

He yawned and stretched. "I called in to the precinct and asked what time your shift would end, and they must have told me the wrong time." He looked at his watch. "I guess I've been sitting here for an hour, waiting to talk to you."

"Couldn't you just call me?"

He was gazing at her so intently in the half light, she felt her breath getting caught in her throat again. Only this time it wasn't out of fear, but anticipation. The foolish hope that something impossible would happen.

"Do you mind if we go inside? It's pretty cold out here lying on the concrete."

"Oh," Nicole said dumbly. "Sure, come on in."

They stood and Nicole led him toward the apartment. As they passed the entryway, she caught the movement of the vertical blinds in the apartment below hers being pushed aside, and her neighbor Anita glared out.

"I'm with her, really!" Ethan called out to the neighbor, and Nicole recalled the near-miss baseball bat attack that had occurred his first time visiting her apartment. "Not a stalker!"

Nicole smiled and waved to Anita, who let the blinds fall back into place and disappeared.

"Whew, close one. That woman scares the hell out of me."

"You're lucky she didn't bludgeon you on the sidewalk."

Nicole unlocked her door and led Ethan inside. He closed it behind him, and when she turned to face him, she was surprised to find him only inches away, his gaze focused intently on her mouth.

"If you came here for a booty call, you can turn and walk right out the damn door."

"God, Nicole. I'm sorry. That's the kind of guy you think I am, isn't it?"

Suddenly her throat tightened, and she couldn't answer, so she nodded instead.

"I deserve that. I've been acting like a bloody ass since the moment we met. I've been acting like one my whole goddamn life. And I'm sorry for that. I'm sorry I hurt you."

"You didn't," she choked out, trying her best to look unaffected by his speech.

"I wish I could believe that, Nicole. But I felt something a hell of a lot stronger than sexual attraction when we were together, and I think you did too."

She shook her head no, her gaze darting to the floor, but she knew exactly what he meant. There was that force of nature between them, stronger than anything she'd felt before. Nearly impossible to resist. Or maybe completely impossible. Maybe that was why she wanted to melt into his arms right now, with only pride holding her back.

"I don't know what you're talking about," she lied.

"I love you, Nicole. I know you're the best woman I could ever hope to have, and I'm sorry I botched up my second chance with you. But I have to ask, can there be a third chance?"

He took a step closer, and his body was almost pressed against her, and there was the force of nature, pulling her to him. Her brain said to step back, but her heart, her body and her soul said to collide with him, to never stop colliding. To never let him go.

God, she was a fool. A fool with little hope of fighting it.

"Why the hell should there be?" she forced herself to ask.

"Because I love you more than anyone else I've ever been with. I'm sorry it took a near-death experience for me to come to my senses, but it did. I never should have let you walk out of my hospital room."

"But—"

"Let me keep going. I'm on a roll. I've been a fool my whole damn life. I thought everything was about avoiding commitment, and that no one was worth getting serious about. I know how wrong I was now. It took falling for you to show me that. You're more than worth getting serious about, Nicole. You're worth risking everything for."

His *I love you* echoed in her head over and over again. He loved her. He really loved her. And he had just said it out loud. She blinked at the dampness forming in her eyes. Because she knew damn well she loved him too.

She'd known from the moment she saw him in that hospital bed that what she felt for him was a hell of a lot more than sexual attraction gone wild. And she'd feared she wanted him far more than he wanted her. But here he was begging her for another chance, confessing his love.

Was it all too good to be true?

He must have sensed the softening of her will-power, because he wrapped his arms around her then and held her against his chest, kissed her forehead, breathed into her hair.

"It's you, Nicole. You're the only thing I want. And I know I don't deserve you, so I don't know how I even got the nerve to come here and beg for another chance. But here I am, begging," he said, his words echoing her thoughts.

"Why now?" she asked, not sure what else to say when all she wanted to do was drag him into her bedroom and make up for the week they'd been apart.

"Because I'm a fool. Because it took me a week of moping around like the world's biggest loser to work up the nerve to ask you for another chance. I was afraid you'd kick my ass right back out the door, and you'd be well within your rights to do that still, you know."

"You're right, I should kick you out the door," she said, the tension finally draining from her body. She smiled, almost laughed. "But I must be the bigger fool, because I don't want to."

He pulled back a bit and searched her eyes with his. "You don't?"

"Don't sound so shocked," she said. "It takes two people to fall in love."

His mouth hung open a bit. It was the first time she'd ever seen Ethan shocked speechless. "You mean…" he finally said.

"I love you, too." She was surprised how easily the words rolled off her tongue, as if they'd been waiting there for a long time, longer than she knew.

"You're not intimidated by my noncommittal relationship track record?"

She shrugged. "I've got a pretty similar record. It wouldn't be fair of me to judge yours in that case, would it?"

"And I don't drive you insane all the time? I thought for sure I drove you insane."

"In a good way," she said.

Ethan smiled the smile that drove her the most insane of all, the one that reminded her how little control she had over her passion for him, and she melted into him. She'd never met her match before, not until Ethan. And she'd never again deny herself the pleasure of a man as perfect for her as him in her life.

He kissed her then, long and deep. She opened up to him, tickled her tongue against his, drank him in as if he was the thing she'd been thirsting for. And he was.

When he broke the kiss, she felt tears streaming down her cheeks, and she was amazed to see his own eyes damp with tears.

"Thank you," he said. "For another chance. This time I won't screw it up, okay?"

She laughed. "Just shut up and kiss me."

Epilogue

Nine Months Later...

JULY IN LONDON WAS a refreshing change from July in San Diego. Ethan had been all too conscious of the awkward weight of the ring box in his pocket all afternoon, but no matter how he tried, the opportunity to propose never quite materialized. Nicole was like a soldier on a mission, touring London.

She had them on a strict schedule. Buckingham Palace in the morning, Big Ben at noon, the Tate Museum after lunch until dinner. He was beginning to feel as if he'd seen more of London in the past three days than he had in his entire childhood growing up in the city.

There was hardly a minute to pause for romantic interludes. As soon as he tried to slow her down, she sped up and dragged him along. He was beginning to think he'd have to propose to her on the Underground.

"Do you want to stop at a pub and grab a drink?" he dared to ask as they walked toward the nearest underground stop.

"Are you tired?" Nicole asked, eyeing him warily.

"Maybe we could put off the museum until tomorrow."

"But we're supposed to do the day trip to Stonehenge tomorrow."

Ethan waved a hand. "Just a bunch of dumb rocks arranged in a circle. Really, the photos are better than the real thing. There's a damn fence blocking the view, so you can't even get any good pictures of the bloody rocks."

"I traveled all this way and suffered jet lag from hell. I'm seeing Stonehenge."

Secretly, he loved her on-a-mission approach to travel, as it was her approach to everything in life. And he loved her. He especially loved that he was her latest mission.

"Okay, okay. But I do need to rest. My feet feel like I've been walking over hot coals."

"That's what you get for being a candy-ass reporter sitting at a desk all day. It makes you soft."

He slid his hand over her backside. "Thank heaven we can't say the same about you. Maybe I should become a cop so I can get a firm ass like yours."

She laughed. "Your ass is fine. You know I'd never date a candy-ass."

He took her hand and pulled her toward the pub on the corner. It was a place he had good memories of, the sort with a pleasant yeasty smell and a funky little four-piece band that played every afternoon and evening. As they entered, the band was in the middle of a midtempo song he didn't recognize, something Irish-sounding.

They found an empty booth and slid in across from each other. Ethan's palms grew damp with sweat, and he suddenly recalled what it was like to be a virgin. Here he was, embarking on something new, something untried, something profound and huge and life-altering.

If she said yes.

They should definitely have a beer first though— or five.

"I highly recommend the house ale," he said to Nicole, who was looking around the place, a vague smile on her lips.

She looked at him then, studied his face. "You look like you're scared out of your mind. What's wrong?"

"I, um, I…"

She raised her eyebrows. "Yes?"

"Well…um, you, and me, we're, ah…" Oh, bloody hell. He was sounding about as articulate as a sixteen-year-old trying to score his first lay, too. Smooth, Ethan. Real smooth.

"I've, um, been meaning to ask… Will you marry me, Nicole?" he blurted.

He'd planned an elegant lead-up to the question. He was supposed to tell her how she was the center of his life, the best thing that had ever happened to him, the most amazing person he'd ever known, and instead, he'd gone and flubbed the whole thing. No elegant lead-up, just the awkward question hanging in the air like the smell of day-old beer.

But she was smiling. Really, hugely smiling. He blinked at the brilliant sight.

"Really?" she said.

He nodded dumbly.

"Of course I will!" She grabbed his hands in hers, then leaned across the table and kissed him as though she meant it.

When they broke the kiss, he sighed.

"You've been poking me with that damn ring box all day, every time we get close. I was wondering when you were finally going to break down and ask," she said and laughed.

"You knew? You knew I was planning this?"

She shrugged. "Trip to Europe, meeting the family, the past nine months of dating bliss. I'm a detective. I know how to follow the evidence."

"I can't get anything past you," Ethan said. "I guess that's the danger of dating a cop."

A mischievous look crossed her eyes. "Oh? I thought the real danger was what I can do with a deadly weapon."

"My dear Nicole, your body is the deadliest weapon of all."

And he was so grateful that she used it on him. Day after day, she conquered him the best way imaginable.

She flashed a devilish smile. "I saw a nice-looking hotel next door. Might be a refreshing change from your childhood bed."

"What? You don't like screwing on my rocket-ship sheets?"

"I want you, Ethan. Right now," she said, and his cock stood up like it always did.

He tossed some bills on the table, grabbed her hand, and pulled her out of the pub lickety-split, toward the hotel. Toward their new life together, where he knew he would take any risk to keep Nicole happy, to keep her satisfied. To keep her, period.

* * * * *

Don't miss the next book in the
LUST POTION #9
miniseries!
Look for
A SCENT OF SEDUCTION
by Colleen Collins
coming in November 2006 from Harlequin Blaze.

RUN, ALLY! Don't be fooled by him. He's evil. Don't let him touch you!

But as the forbidding figure came through the mists toward her, Ally knew she couldn't run. His features burned with dark malevolence, and his physical domination of everything around him seemed to hold her like a net.

She'd heard the tales. She knew all about the Wolverton legend and the ghost that haunted The Willows, an elegant old mansion lost by Micha Wolverton nearly a hundred years ago. According to folklore, the estate was stolen from the Wolvertons, and Micha was killed, trying to reclaim it. His dying vow was to be reunited with the spirit of his beloved wife, who'd taken her life for reasons no one would speak of, except in whispers. But Ally had never put much stock in the fantasy. She didn't believe in ghosts.

Until now—

She still didn't understand what was happening. The figure had materialized out of the mist that lay thick on the damp cemetery soil. A cool breeze and silvery moonlight had played against the ancient stone of the crypts surrounding her, until they joined the mist, causing his body to thicken and solidify right before her eyes. That was when she realized she'd seen this man before. Or thought she had, at least.

His face was familiar. . . so familiar, yet she couldn't put it together. Not with him looming so near. She stepped back as he approached.

"Don't be afraid," he said. His voice wasn't what she expected. It didn't sound as if it were coming from beyond the grave. It was deep and sensual. Commanding.

"Who are you?" she managed.

"You should know. You summoned me."

"No, I didn't." She had no idea what he was talking about. Two minutes ago, she'd been crouching behind a moss-covered crypt, spying on the mansion that had once been The Willows, but was now Club Casablanca. And then this—

If he was Micha, he might be angry that she was trespassing on his property. "I'll go," she said. "I won't come back. I promise."

"You're not going anywhere."

Words snagged in her throat. "Wh-why not? What do you want?"

"If I wanted something, Ally, I'd take it. This is about need."

His words resonated as he moved within inches of her. She tried to back away, but her feet were useless. "And you need something from me?"

"Good guess." His tone burned with irony. "I need lips, soft and surrendered, a body limp with desire."

"My lips, my bod—?"

"Only yours."

"Why? Why me?" This couldn't be Micha. He didn't want any woman but Rose. He'd died trying to get back to her.

"Because you want that, too," he said.

Wanted what? A ghost of her own? She'd always found the legend impossibly romantic, but how could he have known that? How could he know anything about her? Besides, she'd sworn off inappropriate men, and what could be more inappropriate than a ghost? She shook her head again, still not willing to admit the truth. But her heart wouldn't play along. It clattered inside her chest. The mere thought of his kiss, his touch, terrified her. This wildness, it was fear, wasn't it?

When his fingertips touched her cheek, she flinched, expecting his flesh to be cold, lifeless. It was anything but that. His skin was smooth and hot, gentle, yet demanding. And while his dark brown eyes were filled with mystery and wonder, there was a sensitivity about them that threatened to disarm her if she looked too deeply.

"These lips are mine," he said, as if stating a

universal fact that she was helpless to avoid. In truth, it was just that. She couldn't stop him.

And she didn't want to.

* * * * *

Find out how the story unfolds in...
DECADENT
by
New York Times *bestselling author*
Suzanne Forster.
On sale November 2006.

Harlequin Blaze—Your ultimate destination
for red-hot reads.
With six titles every month, you'll never guess
what you'll discover under the covers...

New York Times bestselling author
Suzanne Forster brings you
another sizzling romance...

Club Casablanca—an exclusive gentleman's club where
exotic hostesses cater to the every need of high-stakes
gamblers, politicians and big-business execs. No rules
apply. And no unescorted women are allowed. Ever.
When a couple gets caught up in the club's hedonistic
allure, the only favors they end up trading are sensual....

DECADENT

November
2006

by
Suzanne Forster

Get it while it's hot!

Available wherever series romances are sold.

"Sex and danger ignite a bonfire of passion."
—*Romantic Times BOOKclub*

nocturne™

HER BLOOD WAS POISON TO HIM...

MICHELE HAUF

FROM THE DARK

Michael is a man with a secret. He's a vampire
struggling to fight the darkness of his nature.
It looks like a losing battle—until he meets
Jane, the only woman who can understand his
conflicted nature. And the only woman who can
destroy him—through love.

On sale November 2006.

n o c t u r n e™

Save $1.⁰⁰ off

your purchase of any
Silhouette® Nocturne™ novel.

Receive $1.00 off
any Silhouette® Nocturne™ novel.

**Available wherever books are sold, including most
bookstores, supermarkets, drugstores and discount stores.**

Coupon expires December 1, 2006. Redeemable at participating
retail outlets in the U.S. only. Limit one coupon per customer.

RETAILER: Harlequin Enterprises Ltd. will pay the face value of this coupon plus
8¢ if submitted by the customer for this specified product only. Any other use
constitutes fraud. Coupon is nonassignable. Void if taxed, prohibited or restricted by
law. Void if copied. Consumer must pay for any government taxes. Mail to Harlequin
Enterprises Ltd., P.O. Box 880478, El Paso, TX 88588-0478, U.S.A. Cash value 1/100
cents. Limit one coupon per customer. Valid in the U.S. only.

5 65373 00076 2   (8100) 0 11265

SNCOUPUS

nocturne™

Save $1.⁰⁰ off

**your purchase of any
Silhouette® Nocturne™ novel.**

Receive $1.00 off

any Silhouette® Nocturne™ novel.

**Available wherever books are sold, including most
bookstores, supermarkets, drugstores and discount stores.**

Coupon expires December 1, 2006. Redeemable at participating
retail outlets in Canada only. Limit one coupon per customer.

RETAILER: Harlequin Enterprises Limited will pay the face value of this coupon
plus 10.25 cents if submitted by the customer for this specified product only. Any
other use constitutes fraud. Coupon is nonassignable. Void if taxed, prohibited or
restricted by law. Consumer must pay any government taxes. Mail to Harlequin
Enterprises Ltd., P.O. Box 3000, Saint John, New Brunswick E2L 4L3, Canada. Limit
one coupon per customer. Valid in Canada only.

52607136

SNCOUPCDN

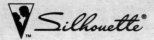

REQUEST YOUR FREE BOOKS!

2 FREE NOVELS PLUS 2 FREE GIFTS!

HARLEQUIN®

Blaze®

Red-hot reads!

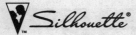
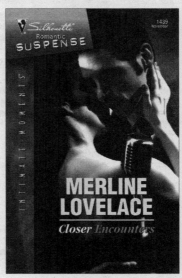

HARLEQUIN®

Blaze™

COMING NEXT MONTH

#285 THE MIGHTY QUINNS: IAN Kate Hoffmann
The Mighty Quinns, Bk. 2
Police chief Ian Quinn should be used to the unexpected. But when free-spirited
Marisol Arantes arrives in town, scandalizing the neighborhood with her blatant artwork,
he doesn't know what to do with her—that is, until she shows him the joy of
body paints....

#286 TELL ME YOUR SECRETS... Cara Summers
It Was a Dark and Sexy Night..., Bk. 3
Writer Brooke Ashby has been living vicariously through her characters...until the
day she learns she was adopted, and that her identical twin sister has mysteriously
disappeared. What else can she do but uncover what happened by taking her sister's
place—and falling for her fiancé...?

#287 INFATUATION Alison Kent
For a Good Time, Call..., Bk. 3
Three dates! That's all Milla Page needed to write a sexy, juicy story on San Francisco's
hot spots for her online column. But was calling her ex—bad boy Rennie Bergin—
to go with her the best idea? Especially since she was still hot for him six years later...

#288 DECADENT Suzanne Forster
Club Casablanca—an exclusive gentlemen's club where *anything* is possible, as
Ally Danner knows all too well. Still, she has to get in, to rescue her sister from the
club's obsessive owner. But when she catches sexy FBI agent Sam Sinclair breaking
in, too, she has to decide just how far she's willing to go....

#289 RELENTLESS Jo Leigh
In Too Deep..., Bk. 1
Kate Rydell is living under the radar. When she witnesses a murder, the last people who
can help her are the police, especially red-hot detective Vince Yarrow. But he's determined
to protect Kate, even if he has to handcuff the sexy brunette to his bed....

#290 A SCENT OF SEDUCTION Colleen Collins
Lust Potion #9, Bk. 2
The competition for reader votes is heating up between journalists Coyote Sullivan and
Kathryn Walters, and they're both determined to win. So what's going to give her the
edge? A little dab of so-called lust potion and she'll seduce him out of the running!

HBCNM1006